OMEGA REIGN

BILL COFFIN

Omega Reign

Reliquary Press books may be ordered through booksellers or by contacting:

Reliquary Press
400 Northridge Road
Suite 300
Atlanta, GA 30350
www.reliquarypress.com

ISBN: 978-1-936519-24-8
Printed in the United States of America

Cover by John Radosta

Reliquary Press rev. date: 08/17/2015

In memory of
the Scarlet Warlock

CONTENTS

We see as our greatest threat the day when our heroes will falter, and we shall be subject to the whims of our villains: the Omega Reign.

But our greatest concern is not whether humanity will remain free, thanks to the heroics of its protectors.

Our greatest concern is that within our lifetimes, humanity as we once knew it will simply no longer matter. For who among us cares for the fate of the anthills beneath our feet?

-Report to the UN Commission on Metahuman Activity, 1986

01
THE END

00:56:21 REMAINING

High above the skyscrapers of Hudson City, Simon Rand held his arms close to his body and dove through the sky, pushing through the sound barrier. The sprawling cityscape below, home to some twenty million people, rushed into a blur as Simon concentrated on his vision and searched the air before him.

This time of day, there would usually be at least half a dozen airliners in the sky, with another ten or twelve helicopters and light aircraft. But now, there was just one, the Apex 2000 Stratoliner, the world's largest passenger jet, on its maiden voyage to the greatest city in the world, carrying with it five thousand men, women and children. Many of them were VIPs of some kind or another, or their families. At least three heads of state were on board, too, though Simon could not remember which ones. All he cared to recall was telling President Carlisle that joining the maiden voyage for a photo op was a bad idea. And now, he was glad the President had listened to him.

The Apex 2000 was flying at maximum speed, the miniature scramjets built into the wings glowing from within as they sucked in air, superheated it, and launched it out the back. Simon knew the craft could go supersonic if it had to, and judging by the plane's level of acceleration, that's what its pilot intended.

Simon listened to the city's encrypted emergency frequency and monitored the air control chatter. He wished he was telepathic so he could broadcast on this frequency, but he was not, so all he could do was listen as the helpless controllers on the ground gave him updates he already knew, and tried not to show how afraid they were.

"Praetorian, this is City One. We have you inbound for intercept. Good luck and Godspeed. We're all counting on you."

Simon heard the whine of afterburners and realized that the fighters scrambled from Merrimack had peeled off. No need to shoot down a runaway airliner when the world's most powerful man was on it.

The Apex 2000 banked slightly and maxed out its thrust. Simon wondered for a moment if it meant to run from him. He knew he could get up to about Mach 1.5, maybe faster if he started downward from orbit. The plane could theoretically go up to Mach 3, but there were those who suspected its hull might peel off at that speed. Somehow, Simon thought that whoever was piloting the plane would not be bothered by that.

Simon pulled to within a few hundred meters of the aircraft and noticed that they were above the business district. The Trinity Towers passed by to the right, down by the waterside, so it was obvious that the Apex 2000 wasn't being aimed at that. But then again, Simon could have guessed. The plane was headed for the northern end of the city, where Heritage Stadium was hosting the Tournament of Champions. There were 250,000 people there, rooting for their country, not realizing yet that 25 tons of aerospace-grade titanium and experimental av fuel were looking to make a very deliberate crash landing right in the middle of them.

Not on my watch, Simon thought as he pulled up alongside of the giant airplane. He could see faces pressed against the three rows of windows, all people caught between the terror of riding a hijacked suicide plane and seeing Hudson City's hero of heroes coming to save them.

Simon focused on one face in particular, a little girl whose parents were behind her, mouthing the words, save us, save us, save us. Simon didn't look at them. He looked at their little girl, whom they should have been consoling, but were too deeply immersed in their panic to do so. She was clearly terrified, but there was a peace to her, the serenity of the doomed, who know that whatever happens next, it's out of their hands.

Simon flew to the hull of the plane and gripped it in his hands, his fingers easily tearing through the outer metal skin and giving him a good grasp. He looked through the window at the little girl and smiled at her. He mouthed to her, it's okay. She smiled back. She believed him.

"Praetorian, this is City One; we have you outbound from Heritage, T-minus thirty. Repeat, T-minus thirty."

Of course, it's T-minus thirty, Simon thought with some annoyance. He knew how long it would take to fly there at this speed. He did it every day. Perhaps instead of giving me useless status reports, you could have tried evacuating the stadium the minute Apex 2000 deviated from its flight path. But no, why bother? What use is there in taking emergency management seriously when you have the Praetorian? Why bother to save yourself at all when somebody like me will always be there when it matters?

Cancel that, Simon thought to himself. Just save the day. You can pity yourself later.

He had the plane in both hands, against his back, straining to powerlift it out of the sky. He flew as hard as he could, pulling up and fighting against the screaming thrust of the scramjets. The plane shuddered against him as it fought both the stress of its engines and that of the Praetorian's strength.

Something's got to give, Simon thought. He could have let the plane go and sheared off a wing with his hands, but there was the issue of collateral damage on the ground, not to mention that the owners of the plane would surely want it back in one piece. It looked expensive.

Simon relaxed and let the plane roll back to its original path right toward the stadium. It nosed down, lined up to slam into the inside of the far side of the coliseum. Simon looked down, and could see tens of thousands of people flashing color cards to write huge messages in the crowd. Right now, the crowd spelled PEACE.

Simon closed his eyes, marshaled all of his strength, gripped the plane tightly and put everything he had into his own speed. Maybe he could get the plane to overshoot the stadium. That was the only option left.

The plane picked up velocity, and fast. So fast that whatever hackware had been used to override the autopilot didn't expect the plane to go faster than its speedometer thought possible. Sensing an anomaly of the catastrophic kind, a deeper layer of security countermeasures kicked in, something that whoever hijacked the plane failed to take into consideration.

The scramjets whined to such a high pitch Simon thought they would explode, but right at the moment of truth, their failsafes kicked in and they all deactivated, putting the Apex 2000 into glide mode. Simon smiled and lifted the plane enough so that all it did was perform a dramatic low-altitude flyover of the stadium. He could hear people scream below, but could not tell if it was out of fear, surprise or excitement. Probably a bit of each.

Simon banked the plane back toward Constitution Skyport and listened to the cheers of relief coming across the emergency channel. He could imagine the pandemonium in the crisis room, the air traffic controllers who would not have to watch the world's largest plane crash into the world's largest stadium and cause the world's deadliest terrorist attack. He could imagine the mayor and his staff weeping with relief, and the respectful envy from the fire and police chiefs who knew they could not have done anything about this, but wished there was more need for their courage.

"Praetorian, this is Mayor Twende. You have a lot of very thankful people over here," came a stately voice over the channel. Then his tone changed, a little more gravity, a little more humility. A little less official. "I say this every time, but...thank you."

Simon cleared his throat and answered. "No thanks necessary, Mister Mayor. I'm glad I could help." By now there had to be directional mikes on him from the ground. There were only about a thousand journalists at the stadium, after all, and half of them were guaranteed to have switched their satcams to track the Apex 2000 once it flew over Heritage.

Or something like that, Simon thought as he switched off his vox. Just another day at the office.

Simon brought the plane down on an empty runway; every other flight pattern in the city had been suspended until this situation was locked down, as usual. Once the plane was safely on the tarmac, the hatches popped open and the emergency evac ramps unfolded. Streams of people soon filled them, and airport security and emergency response teams jumped in to organize the passengers so they could get a reliable head count of them and get them away from the plane itself. It was still unsecured, and while Simon sensed no explosives or other nasty surprises on board, it did not pay to get complacent at this stage of the game.

Simon floated up to the cockpit and let himself in through the main access hatch. The pilots were slumped in their chairs, unconscious but not dead, knocked out by some kind of fast-acting agent. Simon sniffed the air and sensed a trace of an experimental compound one of the Pentagon's alphabet soup agencies had been developing for use in parts of the world with dark, winding caverns sometimes filled with terrorists. Drop a few cans of this in the neighborhood and send in the Marines to pick up the bodies for processing later. He knew it had been used by the covert ops crowd for the last few years, which was part of the explanation for why worldwide terrorism was at an all-time low. The other part had something to do with the government recruiting people during that time between when they discovered they had powers and when they decided to start wearing a mask or cape while using them.

I'm getting off-topic, Simon thought. This knockout stuff was hard to come by, let alone use to put the whammy on an unsuspecting flight crew. Unless it had been synthesized. But by who?

"I know what you're wondering, Praetorian," said a deep and forbidding voice in his ear. "And I know you can hear me; I'm sending you this on that frequency the city uses to keep you informed."

Praetorian scanned the entire console of the cockpit, using his vision to peer through the materials of the plane, scanning its every component for anomalous equipment. He found the gas dispenser hidden in the cockpit ceiling, where the agent could just fall through cracks and settle on the pilots. He also spotted a small computer panel installed deep within the onboard server. He didn't have to focus further and study its circuit patterns to know what this was: the remote piloting system used to hijack the Apex 2000 once its pilots were too unconscious to hit the emergency override.

A $10 billion plane taken over by about $300 worth of components readily found at your neighborhood Circuit Shack, Praetorian thought. Still didn't explain the gas, though.

"Those fools in the military thought they could hide their secrets, but no data is safe from me," the voice said with no small amount of pride. "Were it not for you, dear Praetorian, Heritage Stadium would be a smoking crater. Well done."

Simon shook his head. Why did these wannabe mad scientists always seek him out? If they have something to prove, couldn't they bother the Elementals or Task Force Twenty?

"Tell me about the gas," Simon said.

"Reverse engineering that was child's play," the voice said. Simon stopped paying attention to him, focusing instead on where the voice was coming from. His hearing wasn't quite acute enough to pinpoint the transmission in one go, but he could follow it back to the source if he concentrated hard enough. As passengers continued to get off the plane, Simon leapt upward and bolted into the sky.

The little girl he had seen slid down an emergency slide and looked to the sky to see where the Praetorian had gone. She could not see him anywhere, and turned back to her parents, sad.

Simon rocketed over the city, feeding on the radio signal coming from the know-it-all only too happy to go into the details of chemical synthesis procedures. These geniuses never make it hard, Simon thought. Always monologuing their way right into jail. It's almost like they want to get caught.

It was something that had crossed his mind before, the need for these people to be validated. Most would rather be thwarted and imprisoned than to have beaten their foe without the world knowing. It was why 99% of the would-be destroyers of the world were safely locked away somewhere. And it was why, Simon was certain, whoever made the Voyager disappear ten years ago was in that 1% that was too smart to talk about it.

"You're getting closer," the voice in his ear said, expectant. "I did not expect to stay hidden from you for long. But I have a surprise for you when you arrive." The voice chuckled.

Simon landed on the top of the Glenrock Building, one of Hudson's tallest and most distinctive skyscrapers. Simon immediately looked at the northeast corner of the building, where one of its distinctive stone gargoyles lurched out, away from the building, over the expanse of the city below, big enough to be seen all the way from the street.

I don't have time for this, Praetorian thought. He could hear over the emergency channel that a hostage situation was brewing at one of the big malls downtown. It sounded like Horde was spoiling for a fight. Maybe with a little luck, Iron Will would be on call to handle it. He seemed to be the one hero who had Horde's number; there was a weird kind of grudge match going on between them for the past few years. Maybe Horde was calling out his old enemy for a rematch. It happened a lot.

"Do you know why I brought you here, Praetorian?" the Voice said.

"Because it's the tallest building in the city. Perfect place to bounce a radio signal and waste my time. What are you trying to keep me from?"

"Nothing," the Voice said. "And that's not why I brought you here. I did it because I know what happened at this very spot a year ago today."

A year ago, today, Simon thought. And it still feels like yesterday.

"Tell me where you are," Simon said through clenched teeth.

"You must have saved over a million people since you started wearing that ridiculous outfit of yours, flying around like some guardian angel to the entire planet," said the Voice. "So what happened up here, Praetorian? Having a bad day? Off your game?"

"You had better hope I don't find you," Simon said.

Simon calmed the surging rage within him and focused on the radio signal. It was bouncing off the tower through a relay, and probably half a dozen more hidden elsewhere in the city. He took off at full speed and chased them down, ignoring the Voice's words, pretending he could not hear what they had to say.

"You think I don't know about you, Praetorian, but I do," said the Voice. "I have had nanocameras on you for the last year. I know you never sleep. I know you only visit the Echelon when the rest of your friends hold meetings. And I know that for somebody who swears he's never been in love, you visit Fluke's grave an awful lot."

"Leave her out of this," Simon said.

"Touched a nerve, have I?" the Voice said.

When Simon finally traced the signal to its source, it was in an ugly brick three-floor walkup down in Gearshift, the decrepit industrial district every mayor who ever ran for office in this town promised to revitalize but could never find the will to actually follow through on. One day, I'm giving up the cape and I'm going to rebuild this place myself, Simon thought. But first, some demolition.

He flew through the building's walls fist first, exploding the brick into the grimy apartment within. Simon knew there was a chance the flying debris might kill whoever was inside, but also knew that a guy like the Voice doesn't bring the Praetorian to his apartment without being prepared for a dramatic entrance.

Behind a plasteel bomb shield hid the Voice, who looked like every other overweight computer jockey who spent too much time playing online role-playing games and eating dusty cheese puffs. He had greasy hair, shabby clothes, and his place looked like an entire fraternity had partied in it a year ago without bothering to clean up. The sudden smashing of the wall did not seem to change things much.

"You're under arrest," Simon said.

The Voice looked flattered. "What for? Hijacking the plane or threatening the stadium?"

"For getting under my skin," Simon said. "And for bringing my friend into it."

"Tsk, tsk, tsk," the Voice said. "It's not my fault she's dead, now is it?"

Simon threw aside the wreckage in the room and grabbed the Voice by the throat, lifting him from the ground. "If I so much as blink wrong, your neck will break in half," Simon said.

"I know," the Voice said excitedly.

Oh, great, Simon thought. One of these. Getting busted will be the biggest moment of his life. We have to stop enabling these people.

"So fill me in, then," Simon said. "The Apex was just to get my attention, and the wild goose chase around town was to annoy me, is that it? This is what? All some elaborate death-by-cop fantasy of yours?"

The Voice shrugged. "Only if what I have in mind doesn't work."

"Not very original."

"I don't have to be. Because you are going to retire from the hero business for good. And you are going to hold a press conference to tell the whole world what happened at the Glenrock Tower last year. And then you are going into exile, never to return."

"And if I don't?" Simon said.

The Voice held a small black box in his hand. On the box was a round red button. There were neither seams to the box nor any mechanical parts that Simon could detect. In fact, when he tried to look through it, he saw…nothing. Not the blank spot as if it had been built of lead, but the emptiness that came from looking into space between the stars. Black beyond black.

"If you don't," the Voice said, "then I push this button."

Simon looked at the box. Then he looked at the Voice. Here we go again. Every day, it's another doomsday.

02
METTLE

00:42:02 REMAINING

William Arceneaux watched a large flatscreen in his fortified warehouse, which doubled as both his home and his base of operations. It had been paid for five years earlier by the same nameless billionaire who offered him the chance to undergo a mysterious scientific experiment that if successful, would give him the ability to track down the villains who had done all of those horrible things to his wife. And his daughters.

Five years on, the thought flitted across Will's mind, as it did every morning. So many cases since then. And still no closer to bringing in the one who murdered his family. He knew who it was. There could only be one possible explanation, even if nobody would believe it. It didn't matter, though, Will reminded himself. I know who did it. And that's enough.

The warehouse looked like every other bleak expanse of concrete and corrugated steel in this part of Hudson

City, a huge derelict industrial zone that was home to nobody except a few vagrants, the occasional tourist who made the mistake of getting off the Southland Parkway one exit too early, and Hudson City's most notorious vigilante.

Will never bothered to disguise his place, because nobody in their right mind would come looking for it, and it wasn't like it was the sort of building anybody would just stumble upon. The only times it had been discovered were when villains wanted to hit Will at home, and in a case like that, Will had figured, there was no sense in trying to hide a building from people hell-bent on finding it. At that point, the best thing to do was to beef it up, limit collateral damage, and hope that your insurance will cover the rest.

Will sipped some coffee while watching the morning news. So far, it was lots of talking heads selling lots of news about lots of supers. Most of it was about the throwdowns from the night before. One had left the waterfront esplanade in ruins after the Saurian rampaged through it and then disappeared. Probably in Wicklow Park, Will thought. Another spot was about a foiled hijacking of a military convoy in one of the big tunnels, but the cargo was still lost, so the whole thing seemed to be a win for the bad guys. Still no word on who took the call on that one, but given the poor showing, Will thought it must have been the Hardliner. That idiot was still so green he couldn't make a decent collar if you dropped a bad guy at his feet and gave him a street map to the nearest police station.

The talk switched over to coverage of the Praetorian's flyover of Heritage Stadium; it seemed like most of the anchors, pundits, and freelance subject-matter experts thought the whole thing was some kind of publicity stunt that Apex Aeronautics had arranged with the mayor's office. None of them could put together that

Praetorian had thwarted a very nearly catastrophic terror event. And why would they? When was the last time the Praetorian let anybody down? How could really awful things happen to this city when the world's most powerful man was watching over it?

He can't be everywhere at once, Will thought to himself. That's where the rest of us come in.

He switched channels and came upon another news program that was in the process of wrapping up a feature piece on the one-year anniversary of the St. Patrick's Day bank robbery blitz, as yet unsolved. Will had his thoughts on who had done it. He always did. But Echelon prevented him from shaking down his sources in the usual way. Things were a lot simpler before he agreed to play by Echelon's rules, he thought. But this was still better. The life of an officially sanctioned hero was worlds better than a vigilante beat; running from the cops, dealing with investigative reporters, keeping a secret identity...who needed it, anyway? At least they didn't make me join the team, he thought. Their uniforms suck.

Whatever was supposed to come on next was interrupted by a breaking news story: a group of identically dressed individuals had entered the Monument Heights mall and shopping center and had taken the place over. The news showed clips from the mall's security cameras as the culprits disabled them one by one. They were already knocking out the last camera before there was any decent footage to offer a solid make on them. The last shot was just a second and a half long, but it was all Will needed.

The guys in the mall were wearing strange leather armor that looked like medieval armor designed by a disturbed fetishist. The entire getup looked like it could stop anything up to a heavy caliber bullet, but there was something ridiculous about it, as well. Shoulder pads that were too large. Oversized boots. Elaborate gauntlets with jagged weapon protrusions on them. Genghis Khan at an anime convention.

It was Horde, there could be no doubt about it. Word in the patrol folders was that he'd been released early after being sent up the river for a nickel for his part in the botched Abaldi kidnapping. How was it that somebody like Horde could be such an utter sociopath out in public, but the moment he goes to jail, becomes a model citizen, just so he could repeat the cycle? It didn't make any sense.

According to the few people who escaped the mall before it was fully locked down, it didn't even seem like Horde was there for money. He just came in, duplicated himself enough times to block every exit, killed a few security guards to show that he was serious, and began methodically rounding up every shopper in the place and placing them under close guard by one more of his duplicates in some shop. SWAT didn't dare try to breach the building; anywhere they entered would alert Horde and a hostage would die. There was only one viable option: to call in the one person in all of Hudson City that Horde might talk to first, and that was Iron Will.

Will turned off the flatscreen, zipped up his combat jacket and headed to the motor pool, where he fired up his favorite motorcycle and raced out of the underground garage to the scene of the standoff. He initiated the bike's howler alarm, turning every light green and telling any car with a drive control system made in the last three years to automatically pull over and let him pass. The entire city made a hole for him, and Iron Will made it across the heart of midtown Hudson in about five minutes flat, just in time to arrive on the scene at the same time as the vans from the major news channels.

As he dismounted, he was approached by a harried-looking police officer. "Commissioner Reynolds is looking for you, Will."

"He'd better not complain about my response time," Will said. "I got here before you people even called for me."

The mobile command post was in the main parking lot of the mall, where it looked like every possible kind of emergency response vehicle had been mobilized and assembled at the scene. Police, SWAT, ambulance, fire, even hazmat. Beyond the security cordon, a ring of television news vans were parked, their crews already shooting, their location reporters all moving around for the best background images for their reports.

Commissioner Reynolds stood out from the rest of the cops monitoring the situation. She was tall, blond, and had great features, a supermodel with the heart of a Valkyrie and the medals of valor to prove it. She was vested up and carrying a standard SWAT loadout, and it looked to Will like she was serious about leading the troops into battle.

"You're not seriously thinking of going in there, are you, Commissioner?" Will said as he approached her.

Reynolds looked up from her tactical charts. "Will. Walk with me."

Reynold's lieutenants stepped aside as their boss walked toward an empty part of the parking lot with Will.

"What's going on?" Will said, quietly, hoping none of the news cameras' directional mikes would pick him up.

Reynolds noticed his concern. "Don't worry about them," she said. "We've got a translock on their gear. Nothing's going out without our approval."

Will nodded.

"Look, Will, we've got a situation here. Horde has this entire mall in his hands. At least a hundred hostages. And he's going to kill one every minute unless we meet his demands."

"Killing hostages? Doesn't sound like Horde's style."

"Tell me about it. But he's killed three already. Security guards."

"How do you know?"

Reynolds paused and swallowed. "Because he sent out their heads."

Will clenched his fists. You've gone too far this time. "What does he want?"

"You."

"What?"

"Horde wants you to go in there. Nobody else. If he sees even one of my guys within shooting distance of that mall, he's going to kill every hostage he has."

Will looked back at the main entrance of the mall. He could see two of Horde's duplicates standing by the doors, like grim sentinels.

"This really isn't like him," Will said. "I think the Fugue might have put him up to this."

Reynolds shook her head. "Not again, Will. The Fugue is a ghost story. It can't be behind every single case you work."

"Sure it could," Will said as he walked toward the mall entrance.

"Be careful in there," Reynolds said to him as he left.

Will raised his hand and waved at her, behind him. As he did, he transformed his body from flesh and bone into a statue of living metal, gleaming in the morning sun, bright as chrome.

The two duplicates of Horde approached Will near the door. They spoke in unison. "Glad you could make it."

Will responded by punching one of the dupes with a vicious right jab to the nose and following it with an elbow to the other dupe's jaw. Both bodies shuddered from the impact and dropped to the ground. They began to shimmer and then fade from view.

"We'll see," Will said as he stepped over the vanishing bodies and entered the mall.

Inside, it was quiet. Will listened to his footfalls against the highly polished stone floor, and realized that it was the only sound he could hear. He traveled the length of the concourse that led to the mall's cavernous central hub, and at no point did he see or hear anything.

Horde is in here, and in strength, he thought, but he's staying hidden. This isn't him. This can't be him.

Two more dupes emerged from around corners and approached. "You hit first," they sad together. "That was unkind."

"Then you're going to love this," Will said.

As they rushed ahead, he sprung forward into them. Three bodies collided, Will crashing into them like a flying sledge. Both dupes landed hard blows on Will's midsection and face, but when all of the bodies landed in a heap on the floor, it was only Will who got up.

His body and head ached. Those shots actually hurt, he thought. This is not good.

Another four dupes came around the same corners. "We have been training for this," they said. "You may have iron skin, but we'll make you bleed all the same."

Will took a fighting stance and moved forward to them, step by cautious step. Any second now, another five or ten of these guys were going to flank him. It happened every time.

"Last time we did this, you got to 32 before you gassed on me," Will said. "You train for that, too?"

The four fresh dupes instantly backed off, allowing Will open passage to the center of the mall.

Will kept his eyes on them as they retreated, and slowly entered the center promenade, a huge circular walkway that ringed a courtyard. There were four floors above it. On the ring were more dupes than Will could easily count. He looked up and saw dozens of dupes looking down upon him, filling every ringed floor overhead.

"I guess you have," Will said.

He turned to the four dupes that had escorted him into the center. "So you going to tell me where the hostages are?"

"They are safe," said one dupe.

"For now," said another.

"We have them spread out across the mall," said a third.

"You could never get to them all in time," said a fourth.

"Not before we killed the rest," said the first.

Will nodded. "But this isn't about that," he said. "This is something different. I know Horde. I know what kind of scumbag he is. And for as many people as he's hurt and as many bad things he's done, and for as much time as he needs to do out on the Island, he wouldn't cut off people's heads just to make a point."

"There is always a first time," said every duplicate in the mall. Their voices echoed throughout the silent halls.

"I know you're in there somewhere," Will said, looking at the multitude of duplicates looking at him, an entire army of supervillains. "Just tell me one thing. Did Horde volunteer for this? Or did you just jack him like all the others?"

The nearest dupe spoke. "I don't have to ask permission for anything. From anyone."

"It is you. I knew it," Will said.

"And you'll never live to tell of it, either."

Will smiled. "How many times have you tried to jump into me?"

"Counting just now, fourteen," the dupe said. "You're the only one I can't break into."

"They didn't give me my name just for my skin," Will said. "Better mindfreaks than you have tried and failed, sweetheart. Now either get this show on the road, or let Horde go."

The dupe scowled and reached for Will's throat with both hands. Will blocked it from the inside with his arms and knocked the dupe's hands wide and outside, opening him up to a head-butt that nearly stove in his face.

The dupes gave a collective war cry and rushed him in a mass. The ringed floors above were all connected in a winding spiral that now had become a column of endless Horde copies, running down to meet Iron Will, and break him.

Will ran to the edge of the promenade and dove over it, falling to the fountain on the bottom floor below. His metal form crashed into the marble base, smashing it and sending hundreds of gallons of water spilling out in every direction. Will did not pause for even a moment as he moved to the spot where the great spiral ramp met the bottom floor. The chokepoint.

Will looked up the ramp and saw the first dupes reaching the bottom. They could only fit about three across and still have any room to fight. Time to see if that multiple opponent stuff he had been working on in the Echelon's hazard dome was worth it.

Will caught the first dupe with a straight kick to the chest that knocked him back into others following closely behind. He lunged and punched a second in the mouth while catching a third with a knee to the chest. Each shot was putting the dupes down, its impact going right through the armor as if it wasn't even there. Any normal person would be killed by such blows, their bones shattered, their bodies unable to take the massive kinetic shock. But Horde was more than human, capable of taking immense punishment, diluted with every duplicate he made. Fugue didn't know that, and so it made as many dupes as it possibly could, not realizing it had gone way past the point of diminishing returns.

Will waded into the onslaught of enemies before him, dispatching them with a nonstop series of punches, kicks, strikes and thrusts. He grabbed them and threw them over the side. He pushed them into each other. He went for any opening he could see, eventually striking without aiming, knowing that whatever he did, it was going to hit something.

The harder he fought, the more bodies that fell around him. He realized that Fugue was focusing so hard on bringing the fight that it had not bothered replenishing the ranks. Maybe Horde is tapped out, Will thought. Maybe if Fugue tries to dupe anymore, the host will die. And there isn't a parasite alive that can live for long without a host. That must be where the hostages come in. A hundred escape routes to jump into in the blink of an eye. A hundred escape routes. Maybe more.

Out of nowhere, one of Horde's gauntleted fists caught Will in the stomach, and he doubled over. Another shot clipped him on the back of the skull, and suddenly, he found himself on the ground, underneath a mass of stomping boots. The blows were ringing off his metallic hide, but every one hurt. Each one felt like it was coming through his defenses a little more. One kick caught Will square in the mouth, and for a moment, he tasted blood. He spat it out, and saw little globs of what looked like mercury hit the ground, turning red a second later.

This is how Roustabout died, Will thought. Swarmed.. Dogpiled. Gangbanged.

They're going to bury me in a closed casket, he thought with the kind of serenity he had felt only twice before, each at a time when he was convinced he was going to die in the next few moments.

Something deep within him shot through his sense of helplessness. It almost felt like an electric current, a reservoir of inner strength that told him his pain was an illusion, his weakness a deception. That he was unbreakable. Unstoppable. Unbeatable.

Six dupes flew through the air, thrown clear as Will rose to his feet and heaved aside his tormentors. He swung amongst them with renewed speed and strength, clearing the walkway and tearing into the mass of villains before him, making it up the ramp through them, step by step.

He stopped counting how many dupes he had taken down when he hit a hundred. Horde's going to have a heart attack if this keeps up, Will thought. Too bad, too. He wouldn't have wanted to check out this way. Punked by some ghost nobody knows is real but me.

Near the top, the duplicates became markedly more skilled as they fought, and Will knew he was near the end.

Three dupes stood at the top of the ramp, holding a defensive position meant to keep Will from moving past them. Behind them, Will saw one more Horde take a few steps backward, then turn and run like hell for the far side of the mall.

Will faked toward the dupe on the right and caught him out in the open. He swung left and kicked that dupe over the edge while ducking a mean overhand swing from the dupe in the center. For the next few seconds, the two remaining dupes and Will exchanged a fast flurry of locked punches, kicks, counters and locks. Working together, the dupes kept Will tied up too much to mount much of an attack, and they chipped away at him, hitting here and there, slowly wearing him down.

If Fugue had kept to about six of these guys, they would have cleaned me out, Will thought. Lucky me, I had to fight an entire mall of them.

He let them rain blows upon him, beating him on his head, his shoulders, his chest, his stomach, ignoring his pain until he saw the opportunity he needed. He reached out with both hands, palmed each dupe's head, and banged them together as hard as he could. They went down, and it was over.

Will ran in the direction he'd seen the last Horde escape. He could hear Horde's footsteps ahead of him, echoing closer and closer. He was catching up to him.

They ran through the main concourse and into the food court, where Horde suddenly stopped. He turned to face Will, and looked confused.

"Where am I?" he said, a split-second before Will caught him with a flying arm to the chest that knocked Horde sprawling to the floor.

In the middle of the court sat the hostages, in a big huddle. There had to be more than a hundred of them. Will thought there would have been more. Thank God this happened in the morning, he reasoned, or else there would be a thousand people here. Maybe more.

"Where are you!" Will shouted.

"Down here," said a woman's voice.

Will looked to the crowd, and among them stood a middle-aged woman who looked like somebody's mother. She appeared completely normal, except for the large explosive vest she wore.

Will stopped breathing for a second. He gauged the distance between them, and knew it would take him at least three seconds to reach her. It would take her less than one to hit the trigger.

"What do you want?" Will said.

"To watch," the woman said. "And to know that there was nothing you could do to stop it."

Will tried to calm himself, to find that switch inside his mind that let him turn back to normal. It got harder and harder every time, and he knew that someday, he was going to turn into his metal form and stay that way forever. It worried him.

He made the switch, slowly, and with difficulty, like trying to calm a nauseous stomach. But it worked, and his body reverted to flesh and bone.

Will took a step forward, his hands open and held before him. "You can have me," he said.

"What?"

"I said you can have me. I can let down my defenses. You can jump into me and do whatever you want. Just don't hurt these people."

The woman looked like she was waking up from a deep sleep. She glanced around, confused. When she realized what she was wearing, she screamed and shook in place.

Will felt something come over him, a dream, a voice of his every dark impulse, that thing that told him yes when he knew he must say no. It was in his every thought, forcing its way in, and he felt himself retreating from himself, like descending into a state of sleepwalking. He had become an observer in his own body, and he watched himself look at his own hands, examining them.

Will quashed a small urge to panic. He could come back from this, he knew it.

"Remarkable," the Fugue said through him. "That you would allow this. I expected more from you."

The Fugue walked Will toward the woman. Will watched his body turn metal once more, and his hand reached out to the kill switch in the woman's hand.

"You said you'd let them go," Will thought.

"You're an idiot," the Fugue said. "I agreed to nothing."

If Will had control of his body, he would have smiled. He could feel a flush of arrogance wash through himself, the Fugue's thrill of victory, a momentary lapse in concentration.

Will's sense of thought extended to his every atom and in an instant, he regained control of himself. The Fugue was suddenly a prisoner within him, a dark impulse held deep within.

"You cannot hold me," the Fugue said. It sounded like it was straining.

"We'll see about that," Will said. He turned to the woman. "Ma'am, I'm here to help. Just stay still and I'll have the bomb squad disarm that vest you're wearing."

The woman looked at him with red, tear-filled eyes. "I don't want to die," she said. The rest of the hostages were either silent or quietly crying to themselves.

"You're not going to die," Will said.

"Oh, yes she is," the Fugue answered. "They all are."

Will felt the Fugue expanding within him, pushing out toward his skin. It was so much stronger than he thought it could possibly be, and he felt himself losing grasp of it, like the need to inhale after holding one's breath for too long.

He exhaled, and it left him, and the woman with the vest suddenly calmed, her fear gone.

"If you do this, you'll die, too," Will said, not really knowing if it was true. It was just a theory of Sigma's. There was no way to prove it yet, though.

The woman smiled, and then shook her head. No.

Will grabbed the woman and pulled her in close, turning his body and leaping away as the bomb went off. The blast kicked him through the air, away from the direction he had intended, and he landed hard, his hearing gone, his vision blurred.

He tried rolling over, but he could not just yet. He felt for wounds, but there were none. His metal skin was intact, he was alive. Just thunderstruck from the concussion of the blast. It happened.

He felt a pair of hands help him back to his feet. Armored gauntlets. Horde.

Slowly, his hearing came back, and he could hear screaming and crying among the hostages. Then he heard a voice coming to him, faintly but getting louder, like it was coming down a tunnel.

"…you hear me? Are you okay?"

Will cleared the stars from his eyes and saw Horde before him, trying to make eye contact with him. Will nodded, I'm okay.

"Thought you were dead, man," Horde said.

Will looked for the woman and realized she was nowhere. Just tiny red spatters all over the floor, the walls, him. Already dry and sticky from the heat of the explosion.

"Fugue..." Will said.

"Who?" Horde said.

One of the hostages, a young man, turned and ran from the group, but Will was still too weak to follow. He tried pointing in the direction the guy was running, but it was no use. He was already gone from view.

Moments later, Will was fine. The hostages were in a state of chaos, trying to console each other and come to grips with what had just happened. Will could not tell if the woman Fugue killed had any family in the crowd. It didn't look like it.

"Will, man, I swear I had nothing to do with this," Horde said.

Will looked him over. "I know."

"They're gonna put this on me," Horde said. "I can't go back, man. I can't do it. I got a family now."

SWAT team members ran into the food court, wearing combat armor and leveling automatic carbines at Horde. "Freeze!" shouted the squad leader.

Will watched as EOD technicians also rushed in, looking for any additional bombs Fugue might have left behind.

Will put his hand on the barrel of the squad leader's gun and gently pushed it toward the floor. "He's okay," he said. "He didn't do anything."

The squad leader looked at Will like he was crazy. This was Horde. Of course he did something. If not this time, then some other time he got away with it.

"Are you sure about that, sir?" the squad leader asked.

"I've got Echelon-level jurisdiction here, sergeant. If I said he walks, he walks. Have your men show him out."

"Thank you," Horde said. "I won't forget this."

"Don't mention it," Will said. "I'm serious. Don't mention it."

Horde walked out of the mall, flanked by SWAT gunners.

"Catch you later," Will said to Horde.

Horde took his helmet off and looked over his shoulder at Will. "Ain't gonna be a next time, man. You need to find yourself a new arch-enemy."

Will watched Horde leave, and as he went, Commissioner Reynolds came in, looking at Horde as she passed him. She stopped him and talked to the SWAT guys escorting him out. They pointed toward Will.

"This will be pleasant," Will said.

Reynolds approached. "Mind telling me why the hell you let a mass murderer walk?"

"Wasn't him," Will said. "Fugue."

Reynolds looked at the carnage of the bombing, and at the witnesses composed enough to give statements. None of them seemed particularly alarmed that Horde was leaving, and not in cuffs.

She added it up in her head. As much as she hated to go along with Hudson City's only metal superhero, she knew he was right. And that meant something else, too. Something bad.

"That means Fugue is somewhere in here."

"Yeah," Will said. "Obviously jumped to somebody else when the bomb went off. But we can't tell. We'd have to detain everybody in here until we figured that out. That means you, me, every cop on the squad, and anybody who comes into contact with them."

"Damn," Reynolds said. "That's a slippery fish you got there, Will."

"Yeah," he said. He thought about how he'd trapped the Fugue within himself, and how close he came to never regaining control. It kind of felt like sleepwalking through a nightmare. It was a feeling he never wanted to repeat.

"I'll send over the review files to Echelon," Reynolds said. "Think you can clear the paperwork on this one by the end of the day?"

"No promises," Will said.

Reynolds laughed a little. "Big surprise. Thanks for your help here, Will."

Will nodded. No problem.

He headed out of the mall and back to his bike, ignoring the news cameras and pushy reporters all asking him questions he had no intention of answering. He hit the switch in his head that would transform him back into a normal human, but when he got on his bike, he felt it groan on its suspension. Way too much weight.

That's when he realized he was still metal. He could not change back. But that wasn't the weird part. Every time he transformed, it got a little harder to change back, so he always figured this would happen one day. He just didn't expect it to happen this fast. He also figured it would bother him, not being able to be normal when he wanted to.

I haven't been normal in years, he thought. Now I can stop pretending.

03
BY THE NUMBERS

00:34:19 REMAINING

Ellen Dubrinovich sat back in her large leather control chair and rubbed a hand across the back of her bald head. She was staring at a composite plasma screen that took up the entire wall of the Watchtower, the part of Echelon headquarters devoted to monitoring the wavelengths for signs of trouble. She had sixteen different feeds going, some national and international news, some bringing in intelligence from various top-secret agencies and a few unofficial ones, two reporting the latest winnings according to a classified supercrime betting pool, and the last few were running complex predictive modeling scenarios to triple-check some probabilities Ellen herself had come up with in her sleep the night before.

She was running numbers in her head while watching the screens, and even then, she had a deeper series of equations crunching themselves out somewhere in the depths of her mind. Not even she was fully sure how it worked, but it was that part of her brain that showed her the ways forward, that revealed things before they happened, when they were still in the stage where something could be done about them.

She leaned forward and spared a few seconds' attention on the news that Praetorian's thing with the plane was indeed a terrorist attempt, and that Iron Will had saved those people in the mall. She noticed he had left the scene still chromed up; why had he not transformed back? And were those dents on his face?

None of it was important, though it did raise within her that feeling of sadness that always came up when she thought about the Echelon. Praetorian was the reason for its formation, but he could hardly be bothered with it. Iron Will toed the line only to keep from sharing a cell with somebody he put away. The rest really seemed to need the group, and they were finally starting to come together, but she knew that the great experiment in fighting supercrime had maybe a year left, if that. There were too many divergent needs, too many external pressures, not enough common mission. She wondered if anybody else could see what she did. Probably not. When the Echelon folded, it would take the world by surprise, and leave everyone wondering what hope there could possibly be for a world whose own heroes could not find a way to work together.

Suddenly, she felt a jarring sense of convergence. It felt like a billion-year event, but with the added average probability of a thunderstorm. The last time she had felt something even close to this was when that rogue asteroid crossed between the Earth and the moon. But even then, there was a weird margin of safety built into the precognition. A thin sliver of chance that let her think with honesty that everything was going to be okay.

This was different.

She had to isolate everything she was working on to disqualify it as this Next Big Thing. The first and easiest was the data pointing to an assassination attempt on the President. Even though the chances on that ran to more than 85%, the variance on it was within norms and nothing pointed to any factors that the Secret Service could not plan for, since they had been briefed on it days before. However this one would play out, Korovian rogue elements were the unifying condition, so X them out and everything goes back to normal. Once they finished rebooting the Presidential itinerary, this one would go dark and stay that way.

Next was what felt like an attack on all of Hudson City by some kind of mecha gun platform. Building something that big took the kind of resources impossible to cover up entirely, even with the help of a rogue nation or two. The kinds with the money and resources to fund all sorts of mad scientist pipe dreams. Nations like Korovia. What was the Regent up to this time, Ellen thought. She shook that from her head and focused on peeling this thread back from the main as well, owing to the 99.999% chance that the geeks at Infinite Industries really would get their Halcyon reactor online in a few days. There was Korovian funding there, too, and even though the Regent would probably try to get something nefarious out of that, for now the project was on the level. Time to put the gun platform scenario on ice, where it belonged.

Ellen similarly disentangled the probabilities of a dozen or more other major criminal, paramilitary and terroristic plots that involved Hudson City of the States and her allies, noting for each its chance of redline within the next 24, 48 and 72 hours. None of them had the right kind of signature for a redline event. None of them had anything to do with…this.

Ellen switched off the monitors one by one. I need to think, she told herself. I need to zero my distractions. I need some quiet.

She leaned forward, closed her eyes, and held her head in her hands, gently grasping her skull with her fingertips at the temples. She focused on her breathing, a meditation technique that let her dive deep into that part of her brain that saw everything the rest of her senses could not and never would.

She felt herself slipping into something the opposite of a dream. It was like falling into a room filled with lost things and memories she never knew she had -- too many to count. She felt like she was pushing walls of thought aside, like the growth of a jungle that would swallow her if she stopped fighting it. She watched herself get smaller and smaller, retreating from the vision of herself until she was lost, vanished, gone.

And then it rose before her, something so large that it filled her entire viewpoint. She knew she was pulling away from it, yet its magnitude was so great that it still consumed her vision, like trying to walk backwards away from the sun and expecting it not to blind.

This is what it is, she realized. This is bigger than anything ever before. It changes…everything.

She opened her eyes and calmed herself; she was sweating and her hands were shaking. She took a pull off of the water bottle she had resting on the console and held it against the back of her neck, its coolness welcome.

Korovia factored into every single thread I pulled away from this, Ellen thought. God damn you, Regent.

Ellen spoke, knowing the room's passive mics would pick her up. "I'm going out," she said. "Priority outcomes on feeds two, three and nine. Pull four and twelve back to second level, and normalize everything else. Inform Mountain Top that we've got something big on the way. I'll have more in a little while."

She stood from the console and walked out of the control room, toggling the vox she wore as a necklace. A dial tone.

"Korovian Embassy," she said as she walked past the engineering section. The hum of the cryogenic coolers vibrated in her chest. Anything to keep the supercomputers from overheating.

She listened to the autodial, and then a ring. Connection. A pleasant female voice greeted her in nearly perfect English, with just enough of a Korovian accent to identify it as such. It was about the same amount that 78.6% of all men on the planet found distractingly sexy. Ellen still didn't see the attraction. Sounds like somebody's tongue is sticking to the roof of their mouth, she thought.

"Good morning. Korovian embassy. Would you like to speak to the Regent, Miss Sigma?"

"It's just Sigma, and yes, put me through," Ellen said. It was nice that the Regent finally paid her the courtesy of hotlining her number. After all, forcing a member of the Echelon to navigate through voicemail was more than a bit insulting.

There was a pause on the line. Ellen still felt hot and unzipped the front of her jumpsuit to let in some air. The ribbed tee she wore underneath was sticking to her and as she walked past the training rooms, a few of the new recruits caught sight of her and stared.

Ellen immediately tagged the worst offenders as Razorback, Whipsaw and the Creed. The one called Integral looked and then turned away. At least he caught himself, she thought.

Whipsaw whistled at her as she passed and she stopped, and turned to face him.

"It's not nice to stare," she said.

"Yeah, but for you, I'll make an exception," Whipsaw said. Both Razorback and the Creed tried and failed to stifle approving laughter.

"Mm-hmm," Ellen said, looking them over. She finally focused back on Whipsaw. She took a step closer to him, raised up on tiptoes and brought her face within kissing distance of his ear.

"You're going to die in three days," she whispered. She backed away from him, letting him get one more good look at her before she turned and walked around the corner. "When you're ready to apologize for being a lout, I'll tell you how to stay alive."

The Creed and Razorback said nothing as they headed into the training room. Whipsaw stood in place, his face drained of color.

Ellen's vox came back on as she went up the stairs, to the residential level of the HQ. Her quarters were nearby, a perk of being on the team for so long. After outlasting so many other roster rotations, she finally got a place that was central to everywhere.

"Sigma, how nice of you to call," said a voice over the vox. Middle-aged male, highborn Korovian accent with a hint of holdover from years at Oxford. It sounded like three parts vampire, one part English lord, and one part evil dictator.

Ellen closed the door behind her, stripped out of her jumpsuit, and kicked it into a corner. She walked to her bathroom in her tee and a thong; proximity sensors kicked on the lights and the shower before she even got there.

"Let's not play games, Regent," Ellen said. "I want to know what you're planning."

"But my dear Sigma, playing games is what I do best," the Regent said. "You of all people should know that."

Ellen got out of her underwear and stood naked before the shower. "I'm coming over," she said.

"Then I shall make sure to have a proper reception for you," the Regent said with more than a little iciness.

"It's just me. Nobody else."

"You know, if any of your colleagues were to say that, I would not believe them," the Regent said. "I look forward to your visit."

"Thank you for seeing me," Ellen responded. "Expect me in ten minutes." She switched off her vox and entered the shower. The high-pressure vapor jets had her clean in seconds, but she stayed in for a minute more than she needed to, just to let the heat and the water relax her stiff muscles. Twelve hours in the chair, watching the threads of fate knit themselves together, and now this. I need a vacation, she thought. She replayed the Regent's voice in her head and bit her lower lip as she showered.

Air nozzles in the walls instantly dried her when she got out, and she spent a few moments more getting into some fresh clothes. She picked her dress uniform, as this was as much social call as fact-finding mission. Besides, it took a full fifteen minutes to get into the skintight leathers of her combat suit, and showing up geared for war was hardly the best way to display non-hostile intentions.

She spoke into her vox again as she left her apartment. "Sigma, car for one, launch tube west."

An automated voice came back to her over the vox. "West launch tube, go. Ready and waiting."

Right as the door slid closed behind Ellen, she bumped into Whipsaw, who looked like he was about to throw up.

"I'm so sorry I said what I said and I didn't mean to offend you Sigma and I'm really sorry and I just want to know if you really meant what you said about me dying in three days and— "

"Not now," Ellen said. "I'm in a hurry."

Whipsaw walked alongside her, still babbling. "I know I know but when you told me I was going to die I was wondering I mean I do you know how exactly it's going to happen and is there something I can do about it?"

"Yes," Ellen said. "Stop being such an idiot around your team mates. You might need them someday." And I wonder why this place is falling apart, she thought. These rookies don't know the first thing about what they're meant to do. It's all about mastering your power, putting the hurt on somebody and not going to jail when your antics trash an entire city block. The civilians don't need us. We need them. To need…us.

She left Whipsaw standing in the hall, dejected. "You're not going to tell me what to do, are you?"

"Ask me again in 48 hours," Ellen said, and entered a lift that took her to the launch tube.

She stepped onto a platform with a snub-nosed jet locked in and ready to reply. She slid into the cockpit, belted herself in, put on her helmet and hit the canopy close button. The jet sealed up, the engines warmed, and when she told it to, the plane leapt through the tube, accelerating as it went. She shot out of the headquarters and into the sky over Hudson, the engines burning at minimum thrust; most of the speed had come from the electromagnetic catapult in the launching tube.

The Korovian embassy was on the far side of center city, but Ellen knew she would be there in less than two minutes. She made sure her flight path auto-evaded any civilian aircraft in the lower altitudes, and before she could even get used to the acceleration, her engines cut out and she began the glide into the embassy.

The Korovian compound was the most heavily fortified building complex in Hudson City, after the Island and the Echelon headquarters. Automated cameras swiveled to track Ellen's plane as it came in over the compound wall, but Ellen was sure they had powerful phased plasma guns hidden in them. Korovian miniaturization technology could do wonders; it wouldn't be too much to imagine those things could fire tiny micronukes as well, if it weren't for the notion that the Regent surely wouldn't irradiate his own complex just to defend it.

Or maybe he would. His sense of acceptable losses was…puzzling.

Ellen's jet touched down on a landing pad in the rear yard of the compound, where cloned security guards, each looking identical, received her as she got out of the plane. They were dressed in experimental exoskeletons that looked like bulky body armor. The latest chatter in the intelligence community was that each suit could withstand up to a 40mm direct hit and enabled the user to bench press a mid-sized sedan. Ellen studied how they moved and decided the intel was wrong. These things could press a light truck easily.

"We are honored by your visit, Lady Sigma," said the first guard as he bowed slightly to Ellen.

"It's just Sigma," Ellen said as she tossed her flight helmet back into her open canopy. "Take me to him."

"As you wish. Follow me, please." She went with the squad of clones, who despite their good manners were undoubtedly reviewing whatever assassination protocols the Regent had programmed into them.

Ellen took mental notes as she crossed the palatial compound, meticulously landscaped to look like a little patch of Korovia, cut away from the Vladistadt Foothills and transplanted to the heart of Hudson City. Ellen noticed the rows of Korovian pines lining the walkway. Must be genetically engineered, she thought. Everybody knows they don't stay alive outside of eastern Europe. Something about the rest of the world just did not agree with them.

The embassy house was a classic example of late imperial Korovian splendor, from the last age before the revolution, the counter-revolution, and the Regency. She could not help but admit to herself that these buildings were as beautiful as they were frightening, all strong lines, sharp edges, high, pointed arches. There was something grim and militaristic about it. Something heavy, dark and gothic. And something distinctly Korovian, an aesthetic to be found nowhere else in the world. As if there could be no other country that would dare to admit that the glories of creation and destruction were never more than a single step apart.

Inside the house, Ellen was surrounded by high ceilings, walls paneled with rare hardwood, floors covered in red-veined marble. On the walls hung animated portraits on nanocanvas, oil paintings that showed a slow pan of the Korovian countryside. Somewhere played the

Korovian national anthem, a 90-minute symphony written by the Regent himself. Ellen smirked whenever she heard it. Only the Regent would write his own anthem, and then make it an hour and a half long. It was just so like him.

Down a long, curving staircase descended a gentleman in a dark suit that had to have been tailor cut to fit his tall, muscular frame. He was the picture of Korovian nobility; stark, strong facial features, piercing eyes, and long, thick hair swept back to his shoulders. On his lapel, he wore a pin with the Korovian emblem on it, the heraldic shield of the House of Viriskoya. On his right hand he wore a signet ring bearing the mark of the Regency. It looked like it was gold, but Ellen was certain it was crafted from pure K-356. Shone like gold, molded like iron, and held up to three different memories. With the right electric charge, it could change shape to whichever one the user wanted.

That metal costs more per ounce than it does to put a family into space, and he wears it for show, Ellen thought.

"Sigma," the Regent said, as he came off the final step and extended his hand. "I never thought you would want to visit again. I had imagined that unfortunate show at the UN would have made me too unpopular to merit a social call."

"I don't have time for small talk. I've got an omega event that has your fingerprints all over it. Want to tell me what's going on?"

The Regent's cool exterior changed, and suddenly his face took on a darker expression, one he normally wore when doing business. "An omega event. Are you sure?"

"When it's something this big, the only thing I can be is sure. Tell me what you know."

The Regent walked Ellen to a luxurious lounge, where a staff of clone servants, each a perfect duplicate of a Korovian supermodel template, finished setting down a tea service of imperial porcelain before the Regent and Ellen. Ellen glanced at the tea. It was set up with cream and three lumps of sugar on the side. Exactly how she liked it.

"Please, sit," the Regent said.

Ellen did so, but she never took her eyes off the Regent as he fixed his tea, settled into his chair and took a sip. "You say I am involved. I am curious, what makes you think so?"

"So you're not denying it?"

"I deny nothing," the Regent said. "But I do not take credit for that which I have not done. I am involved in many projects. I am unaware of how any of them, even in combination, could bring about the end of the world."

Ellen leaned forward. "You may be the world's smartest human being, but that doesn't make the rest of us idiots. You know as well as I do that had your crazy ZPG plot worked, that really would have been the end of the world."

"Human civilization, as we know it, is unsustainable. If you ever used your gift to see the future of that, rather than the future of individuals with strange abilities, you would know," the Regent said. "Or perhaps you do, and like everyone else on this pitiful little world, you have chosen to ignore it."

"I don't ignore anything," Ellen said, angry. "And I know the world's got some huge problems. But your solution was to simply kill everyone off and start over with these..." she gestured to the various servants in the room. "...things."

The Regent regarded a particularly beautiful female as she passed by. "These are the templates for a better tomorrow, Sigma. A better species. One that might live in harmony with itself and its environment. Of all of your ridiculous comrades, I would think that you see this more than most."

"I do. But I don't agree."

"I do not expect you to. But it is refreshing to know that there is at least one person on Earth who appreciates what I am trying to do."

"Appreciate? What is there to appreciate about trying to release a global cloud of sterilization nanotech?" Ellen said. "You were insane to think it could work."

"Not in a world with your kind in it, no," the Regent said. "But there are many paths to perdition."

Ellen knew what he was talking about. Korovia was funding numerous rogue technology projects in direct violation of UN directive, but that nobody could find, let alone prove. Meanwhile, examples of it kept appearing in the hands of bad people everywhere. And that was not even counting the genetic engineering efforts to which the Regent himself would refer obliquely, yet never fully acknowledge.

"I will never understand you," Ellen said. "You're giving every rogue element in the world the ability to destroy it. What makes you think that once the world finally burns, you'll survive long enough to claim what's left?"

The Regent raised an eyebrow. "Dear, dear Sigma. What makes you think I won't?"

Ellen grit her teeth. "The UN is going to come down on you again. And this time, it won't be so merciful."

The Regent raised an eyebrow. "I cannot help it if countries out of favor with your own can see a use for my talents," he said. "Korovia is a small nation. Our technology is our only sustainable export. If it helps you sleep at night, think of how I am providing you and your colleagues with job security." He smiled broadly. "After all, what would you do if the warmongers of the world did not have the means to give you such vigorous contests?"

Ellen shook her head. "You're never going to change."

"No, Ellen, I will not." He sipped his tea and looked straight at her. "So you can see why I might find your omega event welcome news."

"So you are involved!"

The Regent dismissed her comment with a lazy hand wave. "If you can call endorsement involvement. I know nothing about this event; I merely approve of it."

"Then we have nothing more to talk about," Ellen said. "Thank you for your time."

"You must know that I cannot let you leave," he said, sipping his tea once more, looking into his cup as if there was some kind of secret unfolding there.

Ellen looked at the cloned servants near the door. They were standing at attention, on high alert.

"Do not bother calling the Praetorian or any of your other associates," the Regent said. "Your communications are entirely useless here. The embassy defenses released a nanocloud the moment you touched down. It is filtering all signal traffic to and from this residence."

Ellen glared at the Regent. "You're holding me hostage? Are you insane? When the Praetorian finds out..."

The Regent clicked his tongue. "You keep using that word to describe me," the Regent said. "It is most unkind. Despite our many differences, I would never use such harsh language to describe you, even though you are clearly fighting to preserve a world doomed to destroy itself. Now, I might consider that futile. I might consider it foolish. But I would never consider it insane."

Ellen scanned her probabilities and saw no nefarious plot toward her from the Regent. There was only an effort to protect, to keep close. But why?

"Care to tell me why you are keeping me here?"

"There are many who presume to foresee the end of the world," the Regent said, placing his teacup and saucer down on the platter between him and Ellen. "You are the only one I will believe."

That was…flattering? Ellen thought.

The Regent narrowed his eyes as he regarded Ellen. "Your ability to discern probabilities is something that has interested me for quite some time," he said. "If I told you how much I have spent trying—and failing—to replicate it on a genetic level, I suppose you would think me careless with my nation's wealth."

"You can't just duplicate a mutation like mine," Ellen said. "I'd think that somebody of your intellect would know that."

"Ah, but you so intrigue me that I had to try anyway," the Regent said, allowing himself a smile.

His teeth are perfect, Ellen thought.

"It would be simple to consider you a probability detector, but there is something to your molecular field that alters probability as well. You cannot leave unaffected that which you observe. By knowing the future, you render it able to be changed," the Regent said.

"That's why I came here," Ellen said. "This omega event...it's like nothing else I have ever seen. I don't think it can be changed. Or stopped."

"I had gathered as much," the Regent said. "And so the oracle has peered into the future and found it unyielding."

Ellen felt her throat tighten. "Something like that."

"Indeed," the Regent said. "Something like that."

"I need you to let me go," Ellen said. "I have to get back to Echelon. I have to see if we can still do something about this."

"You know there is nothing to be done. You didn't come here to stop this event. You came here to be with somebody when it happened," the Regent said. "And yet, if anyone will survive this thing, it will be the one who foresaw it. The one who altered its outcome, even if only by the tiniest variation. That is why I must keep you here. The closer we remain, the better my chances are to survive."

I'm so scared, Ellen thought. He really doesn't have anything to do with this. At least, not intentionally. She imagined her vision of the omega event once more and peered into its endless darkness.

The Regent slowly stood from his chair and adjusted one of his cufflinks before extending a hand to Ellen to help her from her seat as well. "How sad it is that it took the end of the world to bring you back into my home."

...

She moved close to him. Her heart was beating fast. "Tell me you have nothing to do with this," she said. "Tell me."

He unbuttoned Ellen's dress jacket and began doing the same to her blouse underneath. "I would rule the world," he said. "But I would never destroy it."

Ellen was breathing hard, and ran her hands across his chest, underneath his jacket, her nails gently scraping across the curve of his shoulders.

"Not while you were still in it," the Regent whispered as he drew Ellen close against him.

Ellen took the Regent's face in her hands and kissed him deeply, and he returned in kind as they each struggled to shed the other's clothes. The huge windows of the lounge automatically and gradually polarized, darkening them and shading away the view from the outside.

The clones paid no heed to the coupling before them. They viewed it with as much attention as they would spare to the falling of leaves or the drifting of clouds. It was a human variable inconsequential to programming. Nothing to see here. Await further instructions...

No, Ellen thought. She cast that probability from her head. It could happen, but only if she let it, and she told herself she had far too much discipline for that.

...

She moved close to him. Her heart was beating fast. "Tell me you have nothing to do with this," she said. "Tell me."

The Regent sneered. "I would not lie to you," he said. "But it pains me to think someone else managed to remake the world before I ever could. Perhaps you will help me repopulate it."

She slapped him hard.

No, she thought, and cast that probability from her mind as well.

...

She moved close to him. Her heart was beating fast. "Tell me you have nothing to do with this," she said. "Tell me."

The Regent thought for a moment, and then she caught him with a surprise knee to the gut, followed by a close strike to his temple that knocked him out. "You're under arrest," she said, shortly before his clones opened fire on her.

No, she thought.

...

No...

...

No...

...

No...

The Regent looked at her and smiled. "You're reading me," he said. "Trying to see what I might do next."

Ellen felt mildly embarrassed. "I'm trying to see a way out of this."

"And do you?"

She filtered through a hundred possibilities. Then a thousand.

"No."

The Regent bid her come to the window with him. "We could have had this conversation over the phone, or through a video screen," he said. "But then you would have denied me such pleasurable company to watch the end of the world."

Ellen looked to one side, gathering her thoughts. "You're...welcome?"

The Regent looked out the window at the immediate skyline of Hudson City. "Indeed you are," he said.

"Are you frightened, Ellen?"

He knows my name, she thought.

"Yes," she said.

"As am I," the Regent said, his face betraying no emotion other than a cool, detached interest in the near future.

She felt more alone than ever before.

He offered her his hand. She took it and looked out the window with him, unsure of what the next half hour would hold.

04

MASKS

00:27:59 REMAINING

Isaac Arlington checked his things one more time as he packed his messenger bag. Everything was there, but he was afraid that somehow he might forget something vital that would ruin everything and get him stuck in jail or worse. All of his gear was neatly arranged on his narrow kitchen counter, stuck in the corner of a small and cramped apartment.

On the wall farthest from the door, the morning news played on the flatscreen. There was something about a plane and a mall, but Isaac did not pay attention. Just more superhero crap, same as every day. Like they don't get enough attention, he thought. They never show what it looks like after one of their battles; why not spend an hour on that, sometime? See how people look at their masks and their capes then!

Of course they wouldn't, Isaac thought. Bad for ratings. Besides, Hudson City wouldn't know what to do without their heroes, would they?

He looked at the gear on his counter. Well, they're going to have to learn to live with five fewer of them, after today. Suddenly, the sound of a jet plane filled the room, and the apartment shook. Isaac looked out the window and saw the small silhouette of an Echelon jet racing across the sky. Inconsiderate pricks, he thought. With that, any fears he had about what he had planned for the day vanished before a sense of resentment that was never far from the surface.

He powered up his laptop and launched the browser, copying and pasting into a stickie note the date, time and location of the press conference later that day. First would be the official trip to the cemetery, then the memorial ceremony, and then the big press junket right around lunchtime. That's when I make my move, he thought. That's when I get what's mine.

He launched a scanner app for picking up vox traffic and listened to HCPD talking about escort routes to the cemetery and then to Memorial Point. No deviations from what they had been talking about for the last three days. This was a good thing; he had begun to worry that they might change things up at the last second for security reasons, which would throw off his own plans. Then again, the Elementals didn't need the cops for protection. The cops needed to feel important for the day. Changing routes wouldn't mean anything.

Isaac put the laptop to sleep and closed it to conserve battery power. Though it was good for scanning the wireless frequencies and vox chatter, today he mainly needed it to maintain his cover as a journalist. Getting press credentials was easy enough, but nobody took notes on paper anymore. Most just recorded things or spoke into a whisper clip, but a few cut-rate stringers still lugged the old, heavy lappies with them. Usually it was the freelancers, the bloggers nobody paid much attention to. And today, avoiding attention was key.

The gigachip was meant to look like a mobile upload antenna to link into the laptop, but in reality it was a 950 Ghz icebreaker that could break down even an Echelon coded transmission into a simple voice file or text message. Of course, any brute force cracker could do that, but it left a trail that would definitely get the user caught. What Isaac had was the latest Korovian military crypto, a ninja chip that had zero traceability. It cost Isaac plenty, but then again, this was why he had saved every spare penny he had for the last ten years. Ever since the day his father died.

The smartphone was fitted with a separate chip, programmed to play with the timing of traffic signal lights. That bit of work was simple enough for Isaac to code himself, but he took pains to congratulate himself on it. By his reckoning, any grade-school kid with a few spare parts and an allergy to red lights could have figured it out. He just developed the need to do so later in life. Into the bag the smartphone went.

The cloaking device was a Korovian knockoff, so it was going to last for 60 seconds, tops, maybe less than that. And since it came out of some southeast Asian sweatshop, he was pretty sure that the moment he turned it on, it would give him some kind of cancer. But it would also make him invisible for just long enough to get the heck away from whoever might chase him after he hit his target.

The MDS gun was the real prize, though. The keystone to the entire plan, it had taken years to obtain and gotten him dangerously close to getting caught more than once. Ever since Praetorian and the Echelon came within a hair's breadth of invading Korovia on their own, after the UN Security Council decided enough was enough with the illegal nanoweapons exports, Korovian killtech had gotten incredibly hard to obtain. Since the Regent fixed everything he built with trackable sigs, he helped the Echelon hunt down whatever he'd sold, with the exception of a few pieces here and there whose enterprising owners had managed to apply a few aftermarket modifications and render the gear untrackable. Stuff like this went for well more than Isaac could afford, but he wasn't just anybody. He was Skipjack's kid, and he still had his father's connections, even if he didn't have his father.

The MDS was a handheld weapon of mass destruction keyed to specific genetic patterns. The UN wanted them eliminated because they could be made to destroy a specific genotype, for which any genocidal maniac would give anything. In truth, they probably would not have worked that well, since they needed to be tuned to such specific coding that the variation between people of any given race would be enough to prevent them from dying if the gun hit them.

However, the MDS was the perfect thing for assassinating superheroes, Isaac thought, which is probably why the Regent invented it in the first place.

He powered up the weapon, which for its potency was still rather small. It looked like a single piece of ivory carved into the form of a next-generation undercover pistol, compact and slender, made for careful aiming rather than praying and spraying. The power pack was housed in the handgrip and once in, merged so seamlessly with the rest of the body that it seemed to melt back into a single piece of technology.

Isaac activated the targeting computer and ran through its presets.

Preset one: The Deep. Living water. Very difficult to destroy through brute physical force, not so much through molecular destabilization. Isaac imagined hitting him with a single MDS bolt and watching the hero tremble before bursting into a huge splash of inanimate fluid, living no more. This was the easiest, and the first one Isaac attuned. From there, every additional attunement was based off the principles of the first. If this one didn't work, none of them would.

Preset two: F5. As tough as the Deep's structure was for the MDS to process, F5's was even worse, as it could not break things down past the elemental level, and as far as modern science could tell, F5 was little more than a vortex of wind that had somehow gained intelligence and enough power to coalesce into something resembling a physical form. He looked like a ghost, his outline always shifting, but Isaac was certain that targeting his oxygen component would be enough for the rest of him to dissipate into a whiff of nothing. Gone.

Preset three: Bluetip. The last of the incorporeals, he could turn into fire at will, which allowed most energy to pass through harmlessly. Nobody knew why he burned blue, and nobody seemed to care. More than one villain had gone down thinking that hitting him with water or cold would neutralize him, only to learn that he burned so hot, none of that stuff even fazed him. And yet, he could extend a hand to you, snuff out a little of his flame, and be cool to the touch. Isaac calibrated the gun to Bluetip's precise rate of molecular agitation; the idea was to speed it up so that he would burn himself out instantly. He couldn't figure out why nobody had tried it before.

Preset four: Baobab. This was easy enough, since the gun simply had to target that part of her structure that converted sunlight into energy. The shot might not kill her right away, but within seconds, the chain reaction it would start would leave her entire structure burned from within, scorched and dry. She may have been the mistress of the plant kingdom, but nobody trumps the sun. Nobody.

That left the fifth and final preset. Rushmore.

This was the one that Isaac worried about. Of any Elemental, Rushmore was the one who had subjected himself most to science, in part because he knew only too well that it was some unknown science experiment that had created him in the first place. A creature of animate stone, he could break apart and heal, forming new stone to fill in his chips and cracks, though where it came from nobody could say. The prevailing opinion was that he drew it gradually from the dust in the air, building within him a reserve of materials with which he could heal himself. The fifth preset was banking on that; hit the molecular frequency at which Rushmore most probably gathered dust, and turn that process into a runaway reaction that would cause the mighty stone giant to consume itself.

The last one was the only one Isaac was not sure would work.

"Screw it," he said to himself, and placed a Korovian memory spring onto the outer corner of the gun's handgrip before sliding the gun into a holster strapped to the inside of his wrist. Isaac put on his jacket, rotated his shoulders a little so it would hang naturally and comfortably on him, and hung his hands at his sides.

He flicked his right arm, and the memory spring straightened, ejecting the gun from its holster and into Isaac's hand. He was already aiming as the gun ejected, and in an instant, he had gone from standing at ease to having the draw on an imaginary target.

"Bam," he said, then thumbed the preset selector on the left side of the pistol, just above the grip.

He moved the gun a little to one side. "Bam."

He thumbed the gun again, moving back to the left. Target three. "Bam."

Target four. "Bam."

Target five. "Bam." He was pointing the gun at an imaginary figure on the ground. "Bam, bam, bam, bam, bam."

He snapped his wrist and the gun retracted into its holster once more, though Isaac was still looking at his invisible casualty. "Bastards," he said.

Isaac sat at the kitchen counter while making sure his messenger bag was neatly packed before he closed and clipped the front flap. He put it aside, slid a scrapbook across the counter and opened it.

He looked at the inscription on the front cover, well-wishing from a bunch of names he wished he knew better. Most of them were career criminals with bad costumes and even worse names, usually some animal or an obvious play on words. If these guys were more organized, they would have sued each other for copyright infringement, he thought. So many of the names were essentially the same.

He looked at the photo of Skipjack, taken by some freelance photographer for the Midtown Observer. It was the only good one of his dad's entire career, something that his dad was proud of, Isaac remembered. "If they see me, then I haven't done my job," he had said. Still, it was a good shot. It made him look menacing without looking vicious, strong but not lumbering, agile but not wiry. The light had caught every good line of his costume, that stylized flight suit with the trademark satchel and goggled facemask. The picture caught him in mid-leap between two rooftops, his front foot already disappearing as his body began to teleport, while his right arm was only half-solid, just shimmering out of a phase. It was one of those rare times when he was using both powers at once. The Graylight job. $12 million in stolen diamonds from Hudson City's most fortified gemstone wholesaler. They never found the stones.

Of course they didn't, Isaac thought. They all went into me. Clothes, food, a home. Schooling. Books. Music. Opportunities. A life. And one better than his dad had, at that.

"This is for you," Isaac remembered his dad telling him, sitting in his chair, weary and beaten from a job gone wrong and a narrow escape. His face was puffy and bleeding from the lucky shots some cape had gotten in on him. Isaac remembered asking his dad why he didn't just become one of the good guys.

"Because this pays better," his dad had said, in a tone that informed him that was that.

Isaac flipped through the scrapbook, thinking that any detective would give their eyeteeth to get a hold of it. This collection of photos and mementos probably could provide the missing link to a hundred cold case files and pin the identities of no fewer than a dozen black masks. They weren't a formal team, like the Protectors or the Strike Force or the Echelon or any of the others. They weren't even a gang. It was more like a fraternity without a central meeting place, just a mutual promise to share information, to never snitch, and to ride to the rescue when the call went out.

Isaac flipped to the last page, where the photos abruptly ended with half the book still to fill. There was only a newspaper article on the page. Obituary.

Jeffrey Arlington, a.k.a. SkipjackJeffrey Arlington was laid to rest in Endless Fields today. Best known as the super-thief Skipjack, Arlington led a life of crime that implicated him in numerous unsolved robberies. Later in his career, his affiliation with the villain team known as the Deceivers led to his repeated battles with the Elementals, Space Race and the Downsiders. He was slain resisting arrest during the Bayside Riots; an investigation is pending. He is survived by a son, identity withheld.

Isaac pressed his lips together. Somehow, reading it again didn't make it any easier. "Resisting arrest, my ass," he muttered. "I'm coming for them, Dad. I'm sorry I couldn't follow you like you wanted. I'm sorry I'm just another civilian. But I'll make you proud, Dad. I swear I'll make you proud."

He closed the book. "See you soon," he said. He checked his watch, certain that it was time to go. It wasn't. He was now running 25 minutes late.

He swore under his breath over and over again as he franticly slung his messenger bag across his chest, backed away from the countertop, and walked out of his apartment. He did not bother to lock the door.

He could hear the different families making their noise as he hurried down the steps. The thin walls let through the sounds of babies crying, lovers fighting, televisions being played too loudly to cover the other sounds, and stereos being played even louder to cover the TV.

Outside, the sounds of the city formed a more tolerable background. The sound of cars in traffic, people, city sound. It was the constant hum of life in Hudson that natives could not imagine living without and that visitors could not imagine living with.

He looked down the wide street in front of his apartment building, hoping there was not a team of SWAT guys read to jump him. He still was not entirely sure all of that killtech he had gathered got to him without being traced. And as bad as going to jail seemed, doing it before he got a chance to make things right is what really scared Isaac the most.

A large, strong hand grabbed Isaac gruffly by the shoulder and pulled him back from the sidewalk, into an alley around the side of his building. Isaac felt himself spin around and back into a brick wall. It all happened so fast, he had no idea who was grabbing him or why.

"What the hell do you think you're doing?" asked the man standing before him. He was thin to the point of being cadaverous, with dark, sunken eyes and sallow skin. But for as wiry as he seemed, there was a strength to him that Isaac knew was far from normal. The guy looked like he had not slept in days. Maybe he did not sleep at all.

Isaac resisted the urge to flick the MDS into his hand and take his chances using it as a bluff. Maybe this guy wouldn't know it was a specialty weapon. Maybe he'd just see a ray gun and run the other way. Or maybe he'd kill me for escalating things, he thought, which is why the gun stayed in its holster.

"Who are you?" Isaac asked the man. "Are you with the police?"

The man laughed, making a sound like the rustling of dry leaves. As he did, he drew his overcoat closer into him, as if warding off a non-existent chill. "No, no," the man said. "You don't know me. But I knew your father."

Isaac's eyes went wide. "Which one are you? Entropic? Revenant? Skorpius?"

The Cadaver shook his head. "It doesn't matter who I am. What does is that I stop you from doing what you plan on doing today."

The gun up Isaac's sleeve suddenly felt heavier than before.

The Cadaver nodded toward Isaac's bag. "You got anything in there that can't be replaced?"

Isaac shook his head no.

"Good," the Cadaver said. He looked at it, and his eyes glowed red for a moment, and then the bag disintegrated, along with everything in it.

"My stuff!" Isaac cried.

"Can be replaced," the Cadaver said, unapologetically. "You know what can't? Time. And that's what you were gonna do twenty years of if you went ahead with that crazy plan of yours."

Isaac's arm felt warm. He reached into his sleeve and realized that the stranger had disintegrated his MDS gun, as well. Three years of planning suddenly down the tubes.

"How do you know what I had in mind?" Isaac said.

"Kid, you had it written all over you. And the worst part is you actually thought it was going to work. You think a hundred guys haven't tried what you wanted to do today? Guys with powers? Guys with entire governments backing them up?"

"Well, excuse me for being small time, then."

"That isn't important. What you don't realize is that you can't just go after a cape like that. Even if your plan worked, you can't do it like that. That's not how we do things. There are…"

"What," Isaac said through a sarcastic laugh. "Rules?"

"Yeah," the Cadaver said seriously. "Something like that."

"This is ridiculous," Isaac said through clenched teeth. "You think you're helping me, but you're not. I'll start over. I'll do whatever it takes until I get the bastards who killed my father."

The Cadaver took a deep breath. "Look, Isaac, your dad was a stand-up guy. Whenever one of us needed him, he was there in a flash. He didn't have to be. He didn't need any of us. He could have just kept on doing what he did, and nobody would have thought badly of him. He had you to provide for."

"I don't understand."

"I knew your dad better than most. Did more than a few jobs with him. And he saved my ass more times than I can remember. We were all supposed to kick in and help you out when he died…"

"This is the first I'm hearing of it."

"Yeah, well…" the Cadaver said. "Things didn't happen like they should have. Point is, I told your dad I'd look out for you. And to be honest, you didn't need much help. You've been a good kid, keeping clean, working hard. A civilian. Your dad would have liked that."

Isaac swallowed. "He wanted me to have his abilities. Somebody to follow in his footsteps. And I couldn't do any of that."

The Cadaver put a thin, bony hand on Isaac's shoulder. "Don't beat yourself up, kid. Powers sometimes skip a generation. Everybody knows it. Your dad knew it. And believe me, what he wanted for you wasn't all this," the Cadaver said, motioning vaguely around himself. "Sneaking around, getting beat up, doing time. It's a sucker bet, kid. Guys like me and your dad, we don't ever make one last score and retire to some beach. That's just some story we tell ourselves. You know what happens to guys like us? We either die in jail or we die on some corner. That's what we do."

"So is that supposed to make what happened to my father alright?"

The Cadaver shook his head. "Hell no. What happened to your dad was wrong. He wasn't even supposed to be there."

"I wouldn't know. All I remember was some riot going on, and we got a phone call. He suited up, ported out, and the next time I saw him was at the funeral."

"It was bad," the Cadaver said. "Still don't know how it got started, exactly. Both sides lost a lot of people that day. Your dad was collateral damage."

"Collateral what?" Isaac said. He grabbed the Cadaver by the lapels and pushed him back across the alley, slamming him into the opposite wall. "Powers or not, I'll break you in half, you talk like that again."

The Cadaver looked at Isaac's hands, then looked Isaac in the eyes. Isaac realized he needed to let go immediately, and did so. He wanted to find the ability to apologize for what he'd just done, but he was too busy being thankful that the Cadaver had not killed him for his transgression.

"I don't think any of those capes even knew your dad was there, kid. He just ported in and started taking us out of that riot, one at a time. By then, Rushmore and Throwdown were going at it, and I think some flying debris clipped your dad. It was a freak accident, kid. It wasn't supposed to happen."

"So it was Rushmore, then," Isaac said.

The Cadaver took a moment to speak, not really wanting to agree with Isaac. "Yeah. It was Rushmore."

That simplifies things, Isaac thought. I just have to hit him, then.

"You know, it's not like he got away with it," the Cadaver said. "Those guys broke up after. Hung up their capes."

"I'm sure they've suffered," Isaac muttered.

"Don't think they haven't," the Cadaver said. "For those guys, not being who they are is worse than dying. You don't understand because you're not in the life. But Rushmore and them…they got what was coming to them. And then some."

The Cadaver looked out into the street, checking for something, before he returned his attention to Isaac. "I can't stay here much longer. But you got to know something, Isaac. Your dad, he…" He stopped, lost in thought. What was he thinking, Isaac wondered.

The Cadaver started over. "You're a good kid. You're smart. So, be smart. Forget all of this and do the civilian thing. If your dad could have, that what he would have done. And you two would still be together today."

Police cars drove by, sirens blaring. It was the memorial convoy. Looks like they deviated the path after all, Isaac thought. Right in front of my goddamned home.

"I gotta go," the Cadaver said. "Don't make me have to find you like this again." And with that, he turned and walked briskly down the alley, disappearing from sight.

Isaac walked slowly to the sidewalk, thinking about everything the Cadaver had said. He leaned against his apartment building, watching the patrol cars roll past. In the middle of their formation, he saw a series of black SUVs drive by, each carrying some kind of VIP, a hero on the way to the cemetery to pay respects to a fallen teammate who died in the riot. One of the vehicles was bigger than the others. Wider. Fortified suspension. Open top. In it sat a huge stone man dressed in a dark suit. His head had four sides to it, each one bearing the face of an old President. The side with Abraham Lincoln rotated toward Isaac and met his eyes.

Isaac nodded toward him. Rushmore noticed the gesture and nodded in return. Even for a living statue, the guy looked serious, Isaac thought. He thought about the MDS pistol he'd worn inside his sleeve. At this range, it would have been impossible to miss. Could have hit him right in the eye, dead center.

It would have worked, Isaac thought. I know it would.

Rushmore's hummer cruised through the intersection, followed by one last VIP car, then some police backup, and then the convoy was past, on its way to memorialize the fallen worth memorializing.

Isaac put his hands in his pockets, wondering what he was supposed to do now. That's when he noticed the sound in his ears, like tinnitus, only deeper. And getting louder, second by second. Then he could feel it thrumming in his chest. He felt like he was going to double over, and looked up, only to see that of the hundreds of people on his block, he was the only one affected in this way.

It isn't fair, he thought as he dropped to the ground.

05

PUBLIC ENEMY

00:14:41 REMAINING

Darius Green waited for the convoy to pass before he tried to cross the street. He could see Rushmore riding near the back of it, which meant that Baobab, F5, that blue fire guy, and the one who could turn into water were somewhere in there, too. He was glad their group had disbanded. It seemed like every time they brought in some bad guy, they took out half the city along with it. That's just unprofessional, he thought.

Darius reached up and scratched the graying stubble on his chin with one of the prosthetic hooks he wore on the stumps of his forearms. Big convoy, he thought. Lots of unhappy superheroes in it. Never a good sign; every time the capes took the day off, the black masks always tried to make an event out of it.

He shook his head a little to keep one of his dreadlocks from falling over his shoulder, one of the smaller ones that always seemed to fall in his face. Need to tie these things back more often, he thought.

Once the black SUVs and cop cars were gone, Darius crossed, looking both ways for signs of a car chase, or some runaway piece of equipment or other bizarre accident that might take him out. In this town, it paid to be cautious.

He got across safely and entered the corner grocery on the other side. It was a dingy, cramped place, like anywhere else in this section of the city, but it was familiar and cheap and most of all, safe. Ever since Iron Will damn near killed the Repo Man two blocks down, black masks avoided the entire neighborhood. And that meant no capes came around, either. That was important.

"Hola, mister," said the smiling boy behind the counter.

"Hola yourself, Miguel," Darius said. "Here for my weekly pickup."

Miguel lifted a brown paper bag with handles onto the countertop. "Right here, Mister Darius."

Darius looped one of his arms through the handles and rotated, so the bag hitched itself securely on his shoulder. Then he reached into a coat pocket and delicately fished out some bills with one of his hooks. "Here you go," he said to the boy. "Keep the change."

"You sure, Mister Darius?"

"I'm sure. Hey, do you have any of that powder you put into milk to make it taste different?"

"I think so," Miguel said. "Papa restocked last night. Let me check."

"Cool. I'll take whatever you got. I love that stuff."

As Miguel headed to the rear of the store, Darius looked around, warily. No sign of trouble, but still, he had a feeling something was not quite right. Nobody else was in the store, and from what he could see, there was nobody outside of it. Still, that didn't mean there wasn't trouble on the way…

"We only have strawberry," Miguel said, returning to the counter. He held in his hand a can with a pink rabbit on it.

"That'll do," Darius said, rotating his body a little so the bag on his shoulder faced Miguel. "You want to put it in there for me?"

Miguel reached over the counter and fit the can in the bag without smashing the bread on top.

"How much I owe you?" Darius asked.

Miguel shook his head. "Even after this, I still owe you change."

Darius smiled. "Then I guess you've got a little something for your girlfriend."

Miguel grinned. "I don't have one. I'm only nine."

Darius pulled his head back a little and scrunched his face. "No girlfriend? Boy, you better get a move on, then! I seen that Roberta getting all giggly whenever she come in here."

Miguel looked embarrassed.

"Uh, huh. I knew it! Tell you what to do. Take some of that money I gave you, and buy her some flowers. Take her to the park. Girls like that sort of stuff."

"Okay, Mister Darius."

Darius moved toward the door. "I'm serious, now. I'm gonna check up on you." He winked at Miguel, smiling.

"See you, Mister Darius!"

"Later, Miguel. Say hi to your moms and your pops for me."

The moment Darius walked out to the top step of the grocery store's walkup, he saw five costumed heroes standing before him in a wide semicircle. Their formation had blocked off traffic in the street; cars a half-block in either direction had either stopped cold or turned around. They knew what heroes in the street meant.

Darius took a slow step forward so he could let the grocery door click shut behind him. He looked at the heroes before him. None of them looked a day over 25. None of them wore Echelon emblems, either, so that made them a new group. Probably not very good with their powers yet. Probably have something to prove. So why not go trophy hunting, he thought. It's the same damned story every time.

"That's far enough, Threshold," said the hero in the center of the formation. He was tall, broad and muscular, and he was wearing the same kind of tight-fitting multicolored leathers that every hero seemed to wear nowadays, only they each had thin layers of interlocking armor plates on top as well. Whatever happened to the old uniforms? They had more style, Darius thought. These new getups look like something you'd wear to a SWAT team's bondage party.

Darius studied each of the five. The one in the center had the look of a blaster; white electricity was crackling from his eyes and periodically made a kind of Jacob's Ladder between them. The skinny girl to his left was blurring; her kick was speed, obviously. Guy to her left was a little scrawny, so maybe he was a different kind of blaster, or he had some kind of power meant to throw the battle in their favor, though maybe not in an obvious way.

Guy to the right of the leader was a little too large. He was the brick. Girl to his side looked tall and lean, too. Combat expert, maybe? Darius pursed his lips. These kids were already in over their heads. You never put your tank and your fighter that close together. They tend to have the same weaknesses. You're just begging for them both to get taken out at the same time. It was like putting your entire defense on one side; ball's just gonna go around them and make them look stupid.

"It's getting late," Darius said. "You kids are going to miss homeroom."

"Very funny," said the leader. "We can do this the easy way or the hard way, Threshold. Which is it going to be?"

Darius' eyes narrowed. "I don't go by that name. Never did."

"Half a dozen warrants on your ass say otherwise," said the speedster girl.

"You here to collect on them, then?"

"Naw," said the brick. "On the seven figures the Rainmaker put on your head."

"What?" Darius said. "That was ten years ago."

"The matter's still unresolved to him," said the fighter girl on the end. "He's the one stuck in a wheelchair."

"Not my fault," Darius said. "He started it."

"We're done talking," said the leader. "You ready, old man?"

The leader's body armor suddenly crumpled inward, as if crushed by a giant, unseen hand. The leader screamed as his contorted body keeled over. Then it launched off the sidewalk, flying through the air, kicked away. He landed in the park across the street and rolled for a few feet before stopping.

"Yep," Darius said.

The speedster took off in a blur, scooping up her fallen comrade and leaving the scene with him. Moving him someplace safe, Darius thought disapprovingly. Moving anybody with his injuries at speed is just going to jack him up more.

Meanwhile, the other team members jumped into action. The fighter looked over to her scrawny teammate on the end of the formation. "Shutdown, man, come on!"

"I'm trying!" the kid shouted back. Darius noticed Shutdown - what kind of name was that? - was staring at him intently. "It's not working on him!"

Darius felt a headache coming on, and the same kind of lack of will to use his powers that wasn't all that different from the utter inability he sometimes felt when he was trying to paint, and it just wasn't happening. But it was a small pain, and one he ignored easily. Maybe when he'd first found his powers this would have stopped him. But that was a long time ago, and he'd seen and done a lot since then.

Darius imagined a line of force extending from him to the kid, and Shutdown's head snapped back as if punched hard. He staggered back but stayed on his feet, so Darius hit him twice more, once in the stomach, and once across the jaw. That put the kid down.

From the corner of his eye, he saw the fighter launching at him with incredible speed, and he barely got a shield up in time. He could only get a simple panel up, and he had to keep moving it around to intercept the flurry of punches and kicks the girl was throwing at him. She was good, he thought. I let just one of those through, I'm going to spend the rest of the day sleeping it off.

Darius extended lines of force out to the girl, but she somehow sensed that they were coming, and she expertly bobbed and weaved away from them. She counterattacked against his shielding, and for what felt like minutes they continued like this, each trying to find a way to slip one attack through the other's defenses that would create enough of an opening to end the fight.

It had not escaped Darius' notice that the brick was flanking him, and fast. He and the fighter had only been standing off to each other for maybe a few seconds, but in that time, the brick had dashed forward, his hands grasping, looking to crush something.

Darius grabbed the brick with a thrust of energy and threw him aside, where he crashed into the fighter chick. Both tumbled off the front stoop. The fighter landed on one hand and sprung off, twisting in the air and landing on her feet. The brick fell less gracefully and tumbled to the street. The moment he got up, Darius fixed his vision on a parked car, lifted it from afar, and hit the brick with it. The brick looked like he could take it, and the car had been illegally parked in a handicapped spot. It deserved it.

The car smashed down on the brick, flattening him to the ground momentarily while the fighter jumped back to avoid flying debris. A second later, the brick recovered, standing up and hurling the car up and off of him, where it spun through the air, and landed on the park grounds behind him. The few people there screamed as they saw the car coming their way, and two of them had to dive to the grass as the chassis tumbled past.

Darius looked at the car and grabbed it with his thoughts, stopping it and setting it down gently. It was the opening the fighter chick needed to land a perfect kick to Darius' ribcage.

He staggered over and fell from the stoop, unable to breathe. He thought for a second she smashed his ribs in, but he must have thrown up a personal shield just in time to absorb a little of the blow. The longer the setup time, the stronger the shield, and this one had no time at all.

The fighter leapt off the stoop and kicked at him on the ground. Darius rolled over, and her foot cracked the concrete below.

"Kick an old man while he's down? That how we playing?" Darius said.

The girl said nothing but threw a roundhouse elbow at him. It connected with something invisible just short of his face. The impact was huge; Darius could see force ripple out from the point of impact, just as he saw the bones in her elbow shatter. Her arm was locked in that bent position, broken bones raising weird bumps in all the wrong places. The fighter screamed and dropped back, cradling her arm.

She looked at him with rage in her eyes.

"Don't do it," Darius said, but she didn't listen. She screamed something primal and came at him, throwing a straight kick that would have broken steel, had Darius not caught her entire frame and heaved her over, throwing her ten feet into a fire hydrant that broke under her impact, spraying water into the air.

Damn, Darius thought. Now my property taxes are going to go up. Utilities, too.

A thick bolt of lightning scored the wall of the grocery, right above Darius' head. He flinched away from it, and saw the leader of the group coming across the street, firing off blasts from his hands. They were hitting everything but their target.

Darius threw up a shield that deflected the bolts as he moved away from the grocery, but the brick came in and slammed him hard with both fists, throwing him to the ground. Darius pushed him off, keeping him hovering in the air, where he flailed helplessly. An errant lightning bolt hit him square in the back and lit him up, showing his skeleton through his muscles for a moment. Backlit, almost.

That guy can take a beating, Darius thought as he let the brick go, dropping him to the street. He deflected a few more bolts from the leader before he sent out a choke move that strangled him enough to get him to clutch at his neck with both hands. The lightning show stopped, which was mainly the point. Darius kept up the pressure just enough for the leader to struggle and kick, and then finally he went out, too. Darius let him go. He'll wake up with a bruised neck and second thoughts about his line of work, Darius thought. He had it coming, trying to cowboy up on me like this.

The brick got back to his feet, enraged. He looked at his fallen teammates, and then at Darius.

"You best collect your people and skin on out of here," Darius said.

The brick gnashed his teeth so hard Darius expected the enamel to crack. The hero grabbed into the street and tore up a huge chunk of it, hurling it at Darius.

Darius cursed under his breath and raised both his arms. He put everything he had into stopping the incoming debris. He half-lifted it out of the way, and it tumbled to the side, crashing onto the sidewalk.

More pieces of concrete came flying, and Darius could not deflect them all. They hit his shield again and again, and finally, he fell to one side as the brick kept hurling things in his direction. When the barrage was over, Darius looked up and saw that the street was demolished. The brick was standing in the middle of a crater he had made, breathing hard. Darius looked back and saw the grocery store had been demolished, too.

The building was listing, its front corner ripped away by a heavy impact from something the brick had thrown. Darius could see the place was about to fall over, and he summoned what strength he could to shield himself while he moved inside, thinking aside the tumbled wreckage within the grocery.

"Miguel!" Darius shouted. It was dark in the place; the only light left was one fluorescent from the ceiling, half hanging off and flickering.

"Miguel!"

"Mister…Darius?" came a weak voice.

Darius found him underneath a collapsed shelf, his body pierced by a piece of rebar that would have shot all the way through, except it was stopped by a chunk of concrete on one end. Miguel's arm was pinned under a much larger piece of macadam-topped concrete.

The boy's head was covered in blood. His face was smashed in.

Darius shook his head no. No, no, no. Not Miguel. Not him. He didn't do anything.

Not Miguel.

Not him.

Darius carried the boy out of the store while tears streamed from his eyes. But he was not weeping. He was seething. That brick had better be nowhere to be seen, he thought. He better be in the next goddamned area code.

The brick was there in the street, wrenching a piece of pipe from underground to use as a long club. The speedster girl was there, too. Gone all this time, she was now by her teammate, wondering how the hell everything had gone so incredibly wrong in such a short span of time. It wasn't supposed to have gone like this!

Damn right, Darius thought. And now I'm ending it.

He walked toward the brick and the speedster. The speedster saw him and took off, but ran into an invisible wall. It was basically the same trick that caught the fighter, only the speedster was still accelerating when she made contact, so all she got was a stunning knockout, maybe a broken nose. Capes who could move fast like that always seemed to be unusually tough. They had to be, or else the first time they ran into a bug at 300 mph, it would blow through them like a hollowpoint bullet.

This left the brick, who stepped up and brought the pipe down on Darius with both hands. The pipe bent around the invisible dome protecting Darius, and the jarring impact rang up the brick's arms. He let go of the pipe. That's when the brick started to look scared.

As he should.

Darius pushed the brick back into the crater, holding him in place and half-burying him with the pieces of wreckage the brick had hurled about. It was all pushed down by a force stronger than the brick could muster.

Darius picked up everything, every small piece, every bit of debris, every chunk of destruction. It began whirling around him, lifted by an unseen tornado, spinning faster, to bullet speed, past that, into a blur that created a howling sound. Dust on the ground kicked up and followed the vortex.

The brick struggled to move, but he could not. He could only watch Darius walk toward him, bringing the whirling wall. Flying rock inches from his body, the brick held out his arms to protect himself, and his fingers were promptly knocked off. The brick instinctively drew his mutilated hands in toward him, screaming in pain and fear. He looked up, and realized Darius was not stopping.

Within seconds, the entire upper half of the brick's body was chewed apart, eaten up by the flying wreckage, taken apart piece by piece so quickly that there was no blood, just the occasional errant piece of bright red meat, a tiny giblet fallen to the street.

Darius let the junk all fall to the street as he crossed to the far side and laid Miguel down on the grass. He looked up at the news chopper overhead, shooting footage of the whole thing.

Darius regarded the craft and seized its rotors, knocking the bird from the sky. He guided it roughly to the ground, where it landed hard. Probably no deaths in there.

The speedster was coming to, but Darius pinned her down with a thought. She looked to him, saw the torso of the brick jutting out of the pile of street debris, and screamed.

"What do you want!" the speedster screamed. "What do you want!"

Darius looked down at her. "Tell me your name."

"F-Fast Forward."

"No, your real name."

She looked at him as if she could not give out that information. "Sloane. Ortiz."

Darius nodded. "Well, Sloane Ortiz, you and your friends just killed a little boy who was minding shop for his moms."

"I…we didn't mean to. I mean…"

Sloane felt her leg snap at both the tibia and the fibula. The pain was so stark and severe, she just opened her mouth and inhaled.

"You people never mean to do anything," Darius said. "You just do it."

Sloane struggled to keep from passing out.

"Been dogging me for thirty years, and I ain't never started any of it. Not a thing."

"The Rain…Maker…"

"I don't care about him!" Darius said. "He's like every other one of you capes. Figure you'll bring down old Darius, make your name. I ain't anybody's name, got that?"

Sloane shook her head. She didn't want him to break her other leg.

Darius breathed, letting his rage cool a little. "I ain't anybody's name. You remember that, and you tell it to anybody listening. Folks come looking for me, they gonna find more than they can handle."

"I will," Sloane said, breathing hard. "I will."

"Eventually," Darius said. "When you learn to walk again."

Sloane's eyes widened. "No…"

Her other leg broke, worse than the first. Compound. Through the skin, but contained within her tight leather.

Darius walked back to his apartment. He thought his hooks off his arms. No need to pretend any more. Never needed them anyway. Not that it stopped that Vipal bastard from cutting them off, trying to stop my power.

Vipal? Vordan?

He got back to his apartment, confident that there were already a hundred cops waiting for him, but there was nobody. All the heavy hitters probably still at that funeral, he thought.

Vorpal. That's the name. Vorpal.

"Don't bother me," he said as his door closed behind him. His apartment was a modest place furnished by a life of occasional paychecks, the proceeds of some inheritance money, and living like a Spartan. The fridge door opened and a bottle of orange soda floated out and uncapped itself as Darius sat in his easy chair, an old, patchy thing that was broken in to the point of breaking down.

An invisible hand guided the bottle of soda to Darius' mouth and he took a long pull from it. He sniffed and tried to keep more tears from coming, but he couldn't hold them back.

That's when he started hearing the sound.

06

ZERO HOUR

00:05:00 REMAINING

Simon felt the noise before he heard it. His hearing automatically adjusted for it, lest its frequency scramble his brain. It was nothing he had ever heard before, not in the daily racket of the city, not in the quiet rhythms of the wilderness, not in the cosmic gulf of space. This was different. New. Impossible.

The Voice was grinning so wide his mouth was starting to open. He was in ecstasy because he knew the box was working. It was working! And most of all, the Praetorian knew it. He could see it in his eyes, the Praetorian knew. And nothing would ever change that. Just like he knew what had happened to Fluke, just like he knew what had happened before, just like he knew every other dirty little secret he had picked up along the way from the first day he donned a cape until now.

He knew.

Simon looked at him. "What did you do." Not a question. A command.

The Voice could not speak. He could only manage a weird squeaking laugh that seemed to explode from someplace below the bottom of his throat.

Simon increased his grip on the Voice slightly, enough for the Voice to feel it, surely. "I don't have time to be polite with you. Now talk."

The Voice looked back, into Simon's eyes, and told him everything he needed to. There was nothing to say. The box was doing it for him.

Simon looked at the strange cube the Voice held, and he swatted it away, smashing it against a wall. Its casing exploded into tiny fragments, and whatever was inside escaped in a little wisp of what looked like black smoke.

The sound only got louder, and Simon knew that whatever that box did, smashing it had not stopped it. Might have made things worse. It was impossible to tell.

"I swear to God, I'll kill you," Simon said.

"You won't have to," the Voice said, nodding in agreement with himself.

Simon started to panic. It was something he had not felt since his first year, that time when the asteroid got way too close. Something bad was happening, and it was happening right now.

Where can I go? Simon thought. What can I do?

There was nowhere to go. There was nothing to do. And there was a planet full of people he could not save.

Save yourself, something deep within him said. It was not the first time he had heard it, but it was the first time he listened.

He let go of the Voice and leapt upward, exploding through the upper floors of the building, hoping they were empty of people. The ground of Hudson City was a mile beneath him within moments, and he soon watched the sky make the change from blue to black as the planet's surface began to curve.

He could still hear the sound. It was as loud up here as it was down there. And it was getting louder.

Simon put on as much speed as he could and held his breath as he tried to escape the atmosphere. It is getting louder, he thought. It is getting louder.

Maybe it's me, he wondered. Maybe he harmonized my molecular frequency, turned me into some kind of living bomb. He looked back at the planet, huge in his vision. North America's eastern coast was clearly visible where it was not obscured by clouds. From up here, a nuclear detonation would still wreak havoc on the planet below.

Farther out. I have to go farther out.

He put on as much speed as he could. The cold of space frosted his skin and made his eyeballs feel funny, but he kept going. He knew he was a lot faster out here than he could manage in the atmosphere. He just didn't know if he would be fast enough.

The sound was getting louder still. But how? he thought. There's nothing to hear out here.

It's within me, he thought. It's definitely within me. He did something, and I'm going to explode or disintegrate or something else entirely.

I'm so scared.

He thought of Fluke, and how she stood on top of the Glenrock Building. He thought of the last thing she said to him. And he thought of the look in her eyes as she smiled, and said her goodbyes. And he thought of how he could not look at her anymore after that.

I'll see you soon, Jenny.

I'll see you soon.

00:02:00 REMAINING

Will noticed the sound and thought maybe he had sustained some hearing damage during the beatdown Horde had given him. But this felt different, not like an injury. Pretty soon it got so distracting that he had to pull over his cycle and get off. It was just as well; the extra weight he was putting on it was making it difficult to steer, even though it was supposedly designed to carry him even when ironed up.

He crossed a sidewalk, past admiring civilians, and sat down against a skyscraper, holding his head in his hands. The pain was getting intense; there was something seriously wrong.

I'm metal forever, he thought. And more than that, I'm locking up. My blood is metallicizing. My joints will freeze and my lungs will be unable to expand. I am dying by degrees.

As the sound grew worse, he noticed that the headache was just that, and from the sound in his skull. The rest of his body felt fine, already recovered from his battle as always. He felt his head for the dents that had been there before, and they were gone. He breathed in deeply, and had no difficulty doing so.

And yet, he could not turn back into his human form.

The sound had grown into a huge white noise that blanked out everything. Am I going deaf? he thought. Maybe so. Metallic and deaf forever more.

There are worse ways to be, I suppose. I gotta get checked out, all the same. Maybe the Nightingale is over at Echelon. She can fix those guys up just by looking at them. Maybe she can get me right, too. He laughed bitterly and then thought, maybe they can get the Artifex to come over and treat me. Just as soon as he's finished building the latest space elevator or whatever other charity project the UN has him on. That guy really should charge for what he does.

He looked at the people walking by, sometimes pausing to stop and catch a glimpse of him. A few took shots of him with their phones. At least one was a clandestine reporter type who sold sneakshots to tabloids, Will thought. He was sure of it, in fact, and considered for a second whether he should take the guy's phone or simply flip him off.

Let him go, Will thought. There's always tomorrow.

Or...is there?

00:00:30 REMAINING

Ellen looked at Zlodic, who was concentrating on the sound in his ears. "Quantum harmonics, I'm sure of it," Zlodic said.

"Those are supposed to be theoretical. What does it mean?" Ellen said.

"It means you should have kissed me when you had the chance, my dear."

Ellen thought about it and agreed to herself that he was right. It's alright, she thought. He doesn't need to know.

00:00:10 REMAINING

Threshold gritted his teeth and kept up the strongest shield he could, which was pushing all of his furniture toward the walls.

"Coulda sworn the Cicada was dead," he said to himself.

The sound was getting worse. So loud.

"I'm not coming out!" he yelled. "You bastards want me, come in and get me!"

Use some weak-ass sonic cannon on me, will you? These people never learn.

I'm Darius Green. They call me Threshold, but I'm Darius Green.

Dammit, if this is the end, then maybe I should have worn a mask and been the bad guy they always took me for. Would have paid better, that's for sure.

Scratch that, he thought. I'm gonna die a free man. I didn't do anything, and I'm not gonna...not to anybody what don't have it coming.

Come on in, you bastards. Darius is right here.

00:00:01 REMAINING

Simon felt it build to a crest within him, and a calm came over him that he always associated with those aware of the fact that their life was at an end.

I'm ready.

00:00:00

00:00:01...

Zlodic turned to Ellen and arched an eyebrow. "Hmm," he said. "Somehow I expected something more dramatic."

"Like what?" Ellen said. "Nuclear explosions?"

"Not sure," Zlodic said, crossing his arms and tapping his chin as he looked at the Hudson skyline. "I had imagined...oh, dear."

Ellen looked to the sky, where Zlodic pointed with a single finger, and saw an airliner heading into the airport suddenly begin banking and descending.

"It's going to crash!" Ellen said.

Zlodic nodded, watching as the airliner came in low and impacted with the top third of a midtown skyscraper, shearing through its eastern side in a massive explosion. Fiery wreckage showered down to the street as the top part of the building leaned and then crumbled, crashing down into the rest of the building, which collapsed in a huge cloud of dust and debris.

"My God," Ellen said. "All those people."

Zlodic shook his head. "Look."

Another airliner, behind the first, part of the endless chain of incoming aircraft that arrived in Hudson City every hour, came into view.

"I want you to read that plane," Zlodic said. "Can you do that?"

Ellen focused on it, and her eyes rolled back in her head. Zlodic had never seen her practice her craft before. There was something otherworldly about it.

Then her eyes rolled again and she returned to full consciousness. "That one's going to crash, too. And so is every other. They're all going down, and in the same place, too. What is going on?"

Zlodic looked upon the destroyed skyscraper. "That one should have come in on autopilot. I imagine the pilots were fiddling with the controls when they stopped flying the plane."

"Stopped flying the plane?"

Smoke and fire arose from the streets, and Zlodic and Ellen saw the results of numerous car crashes in the heart of midtown. Outside the embassy, the sounds of smashing metal and breaking glass continued as well. Every vehicle, everywhere, was suddenly on a straight-line collision course with whatever was in front of it.

"I imagine every plane heading to the airport will simply crash on the tarmac," Zlodic said. "Each one will simply crash into the one before."

"But why?" Ellen said.

"Isn't it obvious?" Zlodic said. "Everyone controlling them is suddenly unable to. Same with every car on every street in every city in every country, I'd imagine."

"What, are they all asleep? Are they all dead?"

"You tell me, Ellen. You're the one who can see these things before they happen."

"I don't know what I was seeing," Ellen said. "Just that it was bad."

"Come with me," Zlodic said, and he took Ellen over to a large table with a computer monitor built into its glass surface. He said something in Korovian, a code, and the terminal jumped to life. He pulled down a satellite feed of Hudson City.

"Are you patching into the NSA?" Ellen said.

Zlodic shook his head. "This is my own network."

Ellen whistled. "Must have been expensive."

"You have no idea," Zlodic said. He zoomed in on the streets of Hudson's midtown, and saw fires and smoke everywhere. Light aircraft had dropped all over the city. Ferries had smashed into their docks. A massive super-freighter had plowed into the support pylon of the Breakwater Narrows, causing the magnificent suspension bridge to twist, its cables to snap, and the entire thing to plunge into the water below.

But this was just the physical damage; Zlodic was not looking for that. He zoomed in on Central Station, on the city's numerous parks, on its train terminals.

"What are you looking for?" Ellen said.

"It's not what I'm looking for," Zlodic said. "It's what I'm not finding."

"And what's that?" Ellen said.

"People," Zlodic said. "There aren't any to be seen. Anywhere."

00:00:02...

Simon opened his eyes. Still alive. He looked back to the Earth and instantly sensed that something was grievously wrong. He turned back home and soared over the planet, scanning its surface, and seeing chaos everywhere. Every city he focused his vision on was suddenly alight with thousands of small fires and the sudden explosions of movement that betrayed some kind of accident. It was not like bombs falling; the actions were all too small for that. It was like every car in the world suddenly veered off the road and crashed into something.

A sense of panic washed over Simon and he flew low over the Eastern seaboard, scanning every major city along the way. It was something he had done a thousand times before, and every time, there was a background level of activity below. Now, the world seemed like it was stuck between frames. Frozen, inactive. Empty.

He blew through the streets of the cities, franticly looking in every direction for any sign of life. He found nothing. Every city he flew over, and then every suburb, every town, every lonely plot of farmland, it was all the same. Everywhere he flew, there were no people. Not even millions of dead, lying where they had been struck...there were no bodies whatsoever. One moment, the world had some six billion people on it, and the next moment, nothing.

Every living person on the planet, as far as Simon could tell, was gone.

00:00:03...

Will blinked. One second, the street was full of people. Then, like a cheap special effect, they all just disappeared. There was no lightshow, not shimmer and fade away, no dramatic visuals of any kind. He was watching a city full of people suddenly and instantly go entirely empty, as if nobody had ever been in it at all.

Will stood away from his place against the wall and wandered out into the street, dumbfounded. Seconds later, a taxicab plowed right into him, knocking him back as the car crumpled against his metal form. The chassis lifted up on its front end a foot or two before crashing back down to the street. Will extracted himself from the car and watched as the rest of the traffic also went on its way, suddenly devoid of any kind of pilot. Cars, trucks and buses crashed into everything, smashing each other, storefronts, utility poles. More than a few of them caught fire after impact, setting aflame whatever they smashed into. A few buildings had automatic sprinklers to douse the flames, but Will knew that if this was happening beyond just these blocks, the city had a serious situation on its hands.

Will got off the street and listened to the sound of additional collisions and explosions. He watched an airliner overhead corkscrew and take out an entire skyscraper. So it's them, too, he thought. God damn, it must be everybody. Am I the only person left?

He looked at his metal hands, which he could not turn back into flesh. "What's happening to me?" he said, before looking around the city, at the many columns of smoke rising into the air. "What the hell is going on?"

00:00:04...

Darius felt something was wrong and looked out his window, only to see that there was nobody out there. Not a single person. That was strange, he thought.

You know they just setting up to take this place out, he thought to himself. You going to just sit here while they get ready?

"Hell on that," Darius muttered, and he stood from his chair. Moments before, he had been dead set on staying in his home until the police and however many capes they brought with them came in to drag him back to the slam. But something had taken hold of him: to go out and bring the fight to them, to make them regret ever entertaining the notion of trying to cross the Threshold.

He left his place and saw that the entire block was empty of people. Typical, he thought. They cordoned me off. He walked out into the street, trying to sense from where the attack would come. His shields were up; no sense in letting some sharpshooter put a hot one in his brain.

He expected slugs to bounce off of him, but none came. He expected to see shielded SWAT cops taking up their positions, with machine pistols and tear gas grenades and every other piece of gear they could think to throw at him. He expected to hear the bullhorned voice of some tactical commander telling him to be sensible, to give up without a fight, to not make them have to send in the capes. He expected to see a news chopper overhead, so the rest of the city could get live footage of Darius Green getting put in the hurt locker for all those capes he put some pain to over the years.

But there was none of that. Nothing at all. The more Darius walked away from his place, the more he saw that there was no cordon. There was no security area. There wasn't anybody at all.

He walked back to the site of the battle with the bounty hunters and found Fast Forward still on the ground, unconscious. He went to her and telekinetically set her leg. Poor girl was in too much shock to notice it being done. He looked to some small pieces of thin wreckage from the store front, lifted them with his mind, maneuvered them into place against Fast Forward's legs, tore strips off of the costume of the cape he'd killed, and tied them off around Fast Forward's legs, splinting them.

"Sorry about that, kid," he said to the unconscious hero. "Better luck next time."

Darius lifted Fast Forward onto the back of a pickup that had crunched into a telephone pole. He opened the door and sat in the cab, focusing on the vehicle, pushing it forward. Silently, it rolled across the city, where there was wreckage everywhere. He steered it through the boroughs and into midtown, and over to the east side, where the extendable bridge to Echelon connected with the EW Expressway. He got out of the truck, lifted Fast Forward from the back, and gently laid her to rest on the street. If anybody was going to leave Echelon, they would see her. More likely, he figured, there were cameras around to notice that somebody was lying on the ground.

Darius looked around. "I don't know if there's anybody who can see this," he said. "But if there are any of you left in there, know that she needs somebody to look at her legs. They're messed up bad."

He stepped back.

"I reckon y'all got bigger problems than me right now, so I'm gonna head out and stay quiet for a time. You got to come after me, then you do what you got to do. But just know that I ain't got a beef with any of you. Leave me alone, and I'll leave you alone, alright?"

He let his words hang in the air and then walked away, shaking his head.

"You're a fool, Darius," he said. "Ain't nobody around to hear you making deals anyway." He walked into mid-town, and could smell the smoke in the air, the dust from the collapsed skyscraper. I got to get the hell out of here, he thought.

As he disappeared into the city, Sloane Ortiz stirred just a little on the street, enough to know her legs had been set and that she was not where she had been. She had had the strangest dream. She dreamed that everybody just disappeared around her. As she passed back into unconsciousness, certain that one of her friends from Echelon would come pick her up, she found comfort knowing that she had only dreamed it. The world couldn't just go empty in a heartbeat like that, she told herself. It's impossible. Ridiculous. Even for a world with heroes and villains and capes and masks. Nothing like that could ever happen, right?

She suddenly awoke, looked up at the smoking city, and knew her dream was more than a nightmare. She screamed, and not just because of the searing pain in her broken legs.

07

MISSING PERSONS

Three Days Later

"Okay, people, where do we stand?"

Simon stood at the head of the table in the briefing room at Echelon headquarters. His chair had been pushed back and he gripped the end of the table as he leaned over it, peering at the computer screens built into the glassy tabletop as if they might suddenly start giving out new information.

Ellen looked around the table. There were a dozen fellow capes present. Half of her colleagues sitting here she would never have expected to survive a catastrophe like this. The half that she did expect were the ones she hoped would not. She noticed Iron Will at the table. So nice of him to come, she thought. Only took the end of the world.

Will noticed Ellen looking at him, and he smiled in return. Kill 'em with kindness, he thought. The others don't get such nice treatment, though.

A portly middle-aged woman whose uniform looked like a stylized lab coat cleared her throat and began. "I regret to inform the group that Razorback has died of his injuries," she said with the simultaneous twinges of sadness and professionalism one expects to hear from medical doctors. The Nightingale.

"When?" Ellen said, holding her face in her hands. He was that dickhead I freaked out downstairs, she thought. Three days ago.

"Last night," the older woman said. "He had burns over two thirds of his body, and by the time I had gotten to him, he was too far gone. I can only do so much. I..."

"It's alright, Nightingale," Simon said. "Your efforts have been exemplary since the event. Truly, an inspiration to us all. Were it not for you--"

Will cut in. "How many of us are left?" he said, sounding somewhere between boredom and despair.

There was a moment of silence at the table.

"Besides us here," the Nightingale said, "three that we know of. The Artifex is at the Black Arrow nuclear facility, safely shutting down the reactors. Stratosphere is with him, providing transport. And Vorpal was here earlier, but said he had to check something out in the city. I think he is hunting a black mask."

"Like it matters," said a young girl at the end. "The bad guys won. It's been three days and we still haven't seen any people, aside from a few of us and a few of them. That's not even enough to fill a school bus."

"That's enough," Simon said.

"Is it?" Fast Forward said. "One minute I was on the clock, doing my thing..."

"Which was getting your ass kicked by an old man, I heard," said Will.

Fast Forward shot him a look. "Yeah, but you let a civilian die on your watch, too, so I guess we're equal."

"I said that's enough," Simon said.

"I hope Threshold survived just so Vorpal can finish the job on him," said another cape, whose name Ellen always felt was a bit too generic. Redeemer. There seemed to be a lot of capes like him -- stronger than usual. Tougher than usual. Faster than usual. Could fly or swim or teleport or some other ability that got him places. And if he couldn't shoot some kind of energy, then he was able to throw a car at you. The only difference that mattered was why they became capes at all. This was something worth looking into, she thought. Why so many so similar? What commonalities tie them together? Is there something between them and us that decided who stayed behind and who vanished? Why was it that nearly six billion people all vanished in an instant, and yet a handful of the heroes and villains who fought over them were left behind, like ghosts in an empty world?

Ellen was so lost in thought she didn't realize that the argument between Iron Will and Fast Forward had turned into a full-bore shouting match with a few other capes involved. Praetorian looked like he was going to kill somebody. He had called for order and for the first time, nobody would give it to him.

It made sense, Ellen thought. The world really has ended. It's just that not all of us in here have realized it yet.

She had a hard time wrapping her head around it herself. Even with the warning she had seen, it was still hard to imagine that something so huge and so total could just come out of nowhere and change everything, literally, in the blink of an eye. One minute, things were as they had always been, with capes and masks doing battle over who had the right to change the destinies of the billions of people who lived their lives, usually oblivious to the secret wars that raged around them. One minute later, they were all gone. Everyone on the planet, except for a select few people with superhuman abilities, had disappeared.

There was just no reason to it, Ellen thought. There were some six thousand supers in the world, some in costume, some not, some not even aware they had abilities that set them apart. And even among those, only these few were spared. Only a couple of us were left behind. But why? That is the question gnawing at all of our hearts, Ellen thought, and even if we dare not speak of it, we all know it is there. And we all know there is no answer for it. There may never be an answer, and that scares us more than anything.

Amidst the shouting, the voice of the Nightingale came through clear and sweet. Motherly.

"Fast Forward, dear, how are your legs?"

Like that, the argument stopped. Fast Forward looked at the Nightingale, suddenly humble. "Better," she answered, not sure what else to say.

"Perhaps later today we can try you for a run, then," the Nightingale said sweetly.

"Yeah," Fast Forward said. "I'd like that."

Iron Will stood from the table. "I'll be on vox if anybody needs me. There's a city on fire and not enough people to put it out." He left the room, his metal skin gleaming.

"That guy has a serious chip on his shoulder," said a low voice, like grumbling stone, from the far end of the table. It was Rushmore. He was speaking through his Teddy Roosevelt head.

A cape who still wore the Echelon training uniform, and who was sitting next to Rushmore, looked up at the stone giant. "You know, I keep expecting you to talk like one of those guys," he said.

Rushmore's head rotated to the Abraham Lincoln face, and he peered at the rookie. "Four score and seven years ago, our forefathers brought forth on this continent a new nation, conceived in Liberty, and dedicated to the proposition that not all superheroes are created equal."

The rookie looked away, embarrassed. There was muffled laughter around the table, as the rest of the Echelon team members watched Rushmore have his fun.

"Now we are engaged in a great mystery, testing whether the Echelon, or any other group of heroes so conceived and so dedicated, can figure out why the hell just about everybody on the planet suddenly went missing three days ago," Rushmore said.

The rookie was shaking his head. He got me, his gesture said. Walked right into it, too. Never give Rushmore a reason to drop the Address on somebody. The guy lived for it.

"We are met on a great crime scene of that unsolved mystery. We have come to dedicate a portion of Hudson City as a final gathering place for those who somehow survived the Omega Event or whatever the hell Sigma here calls it. It is altogether fitting and proper that we should do this. Because...um...this is where most of us lived anyway, and there's still a lot of free food and running water here. And because I never liked my old headquarters."

There was more laughter from around the table, and once the rookie began clapping, so did everyone else. Rushmore nodded in acknowledgment.

"So...you don't think this is permanent?" asked the rookie.

"Think what is permanent? This situation?" Rushmore said.

"Yeah," the rookie said, suddenly unsure of himself. "I mean, what if it stays like this? What if we haven't been pushed aside in time or phased to another pocket dimension or something? What if something really happened to everybody, and we really are the only ones left on the planet?"

Rushmore shrugged, the cracks in his stone form grinding slightly against each other. "Kid, I've seen a lot of crazy people do a lot of crazy things that put a lot of people in danger. For all I know, this is just some big mind game the Dreamweaver's laying on us, to make us think everybody just disappeared. Or maybe that knucklehead over in Transylvanialand across town lost control of one of his little science experiments."

"He's called the Regent," Ellen said.

Rushmore rolled his eyes. "Whatever. Point is, something big happened, and we don't know what it really is. One of us will figure it out. We always do. And then the people will come back and life will go on, and we'll all look back at this in a year and laugh about it."

"But our young friend has a point, Rushmore," Nightingale said. "If, just if, this is something that cannot be undone, well...what then?"

There was silence at the table. All attention was focused on Rushmore as he thought. Even the Praetorian was watching.

Rushmore's head rotated to the George Washington face. "Then we keep on keeping on."

Nervous laughter broke out. Did Rushmore just brush off the end of the world?

"I think what Rushmore is trying to say..." Simon began, but was interrupted by Rushmore.

"What I'm trying to say is that everybody else on the planet was never more than one bad day away from having no more days, period," Rushmore said. "Why should we be any different? I mean, how many people were out there on any given day trying to blow things up? How many people have we, in this room alone, put away for trying to tear the world in half? How many plots have we stopped just in the nick of time? Guys, I don't want to rain on anybody's parade, but maybe this is just the law of averages. Maybe, given enough time, something really bad was bound to get through, you know?"

"And you're saying that this might be it?" Nightingale asked.

"Yeah," Rushmore said. "Something like that."

Ellen broke the silence that followed. "He's right, you know."

Simon looked at her. "What do you see, Sigma?"

"Nothing," Ellen said. "And believe me, I've been looking. I've been looking and searching and analyzing until my head hurts for the last three days, and I don't see anything. Not a damned thing."

At last, Simon took a chair and sat down, leaning back. "How can that be? In all the years we worked together, you have never had a blank spot. There is always something on the horizon."

"Not at the moment," she said. "It's like I've told you. Right before the event, I saw it, and it was like nothing I'd ever seen before. It was...I can't really describe it. It was just beyond any context for the future I had ever processed. It was as unstoppable as it was sudden. Like an earthquake. A billion-year event. And ever since, things have been really quiet."

"Almost too quiet," Simon said thoughtfully.

Rushmore shook his head. "Only a matter of time before he said it," he said to himself.

"Perhaps we should pay your friend the Regent a visit," Simon said. "See what he knows."

"I've already spoken with him," Ellen said. "I don't think he had anything to do..."

"The Regent always has something to do with it," Simon stated, declaring victory in the argument before it even started. "He's hiding something. From all of us. Even from you, Sigma."

"I doubt it," Ellen said.

"It's possible though, right?" said Rushmore. "I mean there were a few times something got past you. Dreamweaver did it twice, and we know she's still kicking around this damned city because Will laid eyes on her."

"Will says a lot," Ellen said.

"Indeed he does," Simon said. "But I, too, have reason to believe Dreamweaver is active, and we can't discount her ability to alter our perceptions of reality, so until we detain her..."

"Detain her?" Ellen said. "But she isn't wanted for anything."

Simon laughed. "Look around you, Sigma. She's wanted for this. They all are. Every black mask that survived and isn't in lockdown. Until we get the answers we're looking for, our first priority is to clear the city of masks and figure out what they know."

"That'll take some doing," Rushmore said. "Hudson's ten times bigger than before. A thousand. Without people to tip us off, these masks could be anywhere. And last I checked, the Beacon didn't make it, so we don't have anybody who can just home in on these people."

"We know the Saurian is still in Memorial Park," Simon said. "That's where it was last seen after E-day, and that's where you'll begin looking for him."

"Me?" Rushmore said.

"You. I am going to make one more orbital run and see if I can't pick up any stray emergency signal traffic. There might still be a few remaining survivors elsewhere in the world. If I can find them, I'll bring them here to Hudson. We need to gather what resources we have left if we are to figure out what happened, find those responsible, fix the damage, and bring the culprits to justice."

"Sounds like a tall order," Rushmore said.

"Our tallest yet," Simon said. "But this is what we are here to do, people. There are six billion people depending on us to set things right. Now let's get to work."

Everybody stood from their chairs.

"Nightingale, I need you on standby in sickbay in case I bring in any wounded, or in case anybody comes in. Keep me posted on vox if you find anything interesting."

"Yes, Praetorian," Nightingale said.

"And...I need you to do an autopsy on Razorback. See if there is anything unusual about him, post-mortem."

"Are you sure that is necessary?" Nightingale said. "His death seemed perfectly ordinary to me. He burned to death trying to stop a rather large fire. There is nothing strange about that."

"I know," Simon said. "But just do it, all the same. If we're out of dimensional phase, there might be some kind of sign. Or if this is an illusion, Dreamweaver might not have the mental ability to keep you deceived while you're working on Razorback."

Nightingale nodded.

"Ellen, I need you to come up with a plan for how we're going to reach the Regent. I have tried to fly to his compound twice and each time, I run into some kind of force field. I think it's attuned to my specific molecular energy signature. We need to make him talk."

"We could try asking him nicely," Ellen said.

"This is no time to be naive," Simon said. "As for the rest of you, there is a target roster in the Echelon database that I updated this morning. Pick a target whose Echelon rating is within plus or minus five of your own, and start searching. Keep your vox on at all times. We don't have enough people to go in pairs, so be especially careful out there. The entire city should be considered a red zone. Understood?"

"Yes, sir," said the team at the table. Ellen, Rushmore and Nightingale said it, too.

"Then let's go to work," Simon said. "Maybe today we'll get lucky."

08
CATCH & RELEASE

Not likely, Rushmore thought as he left the briefing room. The mood in the building was unlike it had ever been before. He remembered when the Doomscryers raided the building and left it a burning hulk. Three Echelon rookies had died, and even though nobody really thought the Doomscryers would be found, let along brought in, there was a unifying sense of purpose. The Echelon didn't just have to get the bad guys. It had to let bad guys everywhere know that nobody can raid the Big E and get away with it. Not without paying, big time.

But that was just a bad tactical situation. The Big E got hit first, and we weren't used to it, Rushmore thought. Just proved there was a first time for everything, and anybody who belongs in this game can bounce back from that. That riot last year, though, that was something else. That was the kind of thing that made people quit. On both sides.

Nobody really seemed to know what touched it off. There was a pretty bad throwdown near the crosstown interchange, where I-30 and the Northbrook Extension come together in that mad collection of on-ramps, off-ramps and crossovers that commuters liked to call the Spaghetti Bowl. Word on the channels was that some newcomer called Daisy Cutter threatened to blow up the Bowl at rush hour unless her demands were met. Rushmore thought of the initial chatter when the demand came in, and it seemed like just another demand from just another mask who figured that, despite the fact this kind of thing had been tried and foiled a hundred times before, somehow this time would be different.

A bunch of capes responded to the scene and a bunch of masks came around as backup and before anybody knew it, there was a battle royale going on amid 250 cars, trucks and commuter buses filled with terrified civilians, all hoping that they wouldn't become collateral damage in the worst super-brawl since the Echelon was formed back in the 60s, in part to prevent this kind of thing from happening.

Rushmore thought of the battle, of how he'd taken down three heavy hitters he'd never seen before, some blaster named Natural Twenty and some crazy martial artist who could actually break stone with his hands without breaking a sweat. He thought of how he saw Fluke enter the fray, leaping, spinning and cartwheeling her way through it all, busting out that crazy freestyle fighting of hers that would eventually become the model for the Echelon hand-to-hand system. Everywhere she went, the battle went her way. And how could it not? That was why she became a cape; she was Fluke, the luckiest woman in the world. Sigma tried to explain that it was some kind of weird probability field around her that responded to her subconscious, but all Rushmore cared to remember was that she was a walking rabbit's foot when everybody who mattered needed it most.

She wasn't the most powerful cape in town. That was Praetorian, obviously. Well, after Voyager vanished back in the late 90s, anyway. And Fluke wasn't the most experienced, either. That was Clandestine, before he retired. That crafty bastard was so good, nobody ever knew who he really was. He just signed off, left his mask at Echelon, and nobody ever saw him again. That cape had style.

But what Fluke had was popularity. She always looked fantastic. Everything always went her way. She always knew what to say. The cameras loved her. Hell, even the black masks didn't mind getting collared by her, half the time. Some of them even went out of their way just to match up with her. It was like the good guy, bad guy version of junior high. Misunderstood but secretly likeable misanthrope asks out the sweet but unreachable cheerleader. What a bunch of suckers, Rushmore thought. Kind of makes me glad I got cooked up in somebody's secret laboratory.

Rushmore walked to the edge of the Echelon campus, which was on a thin sliver of an island in the middle of the Crescent River. An extendable bridge connected it to the boroughs on either side of the water, but right now, only the bridge to midtown was open. Rushmore couldn't quite figure why nobody would extend the bridge over to Harbinger Harbor. It wasn't like there were zombies over there. Though it would be kind of cool if there were, Rushmore thought. There hasn't been a good zombie breakout in a long time. That Halloween incident two years back didn't count.

On the far side of the bridge, Rushmore saw the wreckage that the Omega Event had wrought upon midtown. When the Omega Event happened, a hundred thousand cars, trucks, boats and light aircraft, in motion, suddenly had no pilots, and the crash damage alone was enough to set a good portion of the city on fire. Once a few gas lines were ruptured, entire buildings went up, and it took the Artifex a full day to get things locked down. That's when Supersonic took him to the other big cities of the world, to try saving what was left of them.

The first few blocks into midtown looked like a major riot had occurred. It brought him back to the last time he ever saw Fluke alive. It was during that throwdown in the Spaghetti Bowl, and she was putting the hurt on some fool who looked like a walking tiger, when Daisy Cutter made her appearance. Fluke immediately put in a lucky shot that KOed the tiger man and went for Daisy Cutter. Rushmore got blindsided by a barrage of miniature meteors from the Krakatoan, and by the time he'd cleared his eyes of volcanic ash, he saw the burning hulk of a school bus, all blown to hell. Fluke stood before it, looking dumbstruck.

There were forty grade-schoolers from out of town in there. Field trip.

Rushmore saw a pileup of vehicles clogging an entire intersection. Every single storefront within a block of the four-way had a vehicle crashed through it. For a moment, Rushmore was thankful there weren't any people in all of those cars, until he remembered why the cars crashed in the first place.

Tumbled vehicles were just the start of it, Rushmore remembered the Artifex saying. There were nuclear power plants across the world that had to be shut down before they went critical. They could only run themselves for a few days before they got into danger. The Artifex said he could handle it, so long as Supersonic could give him a lift. Rushmore had his doubts.

He walked past the remains of a supermarket. Where will the food come from? Where will clean water come from? How are they all going to live? He kept these questions running through his head. I'm the last one who needs to ask about this stuff, he thought. I don't even need to eat. But there are going to be some hungry people when all of the pre-made stuff runs out. Better hope the Harvestman made it through and is off growing vegetables somewhere. Or maybe Biosphere. But she was always talking about repairing the Amazon. If she made it, she's probably down there, all by herself and happier than she's ever been before.

The walk through the empty blocks of the quiet city was like the time there was a blackout for three days, and people stayed inside for all that time. It was such an unusual time. So quiet. So still. It would be nice, Rushmore thought, if when the people came back, the city could somehow stay this way. Of course, without all of the crashed cars and messed up buildings. It sure was nice to be able to walk up the middle of the street and not have to worry about crashing some cabbie's ride.

Rushmore kept going, across town, climbing the hills of Avenues F through the beginning of the alphabet, until he reached the top of the East Highlands, where Hudson City's rich and famous lived in partial seclusion from the regular folks of the city. From up here, they could see the city from a safe distance, even though they were still part of it. It was an illusion of distance that led to more than a few rude surprises when something ended up breaking the glass. It happened often enough that they eventually built safety awnings to catch the shards when they fell.

Things looked pretty good up here, mainly because the people who lived here tended to have drivers and were already where they wanted to go by the time the Event went down. There were a few buildings that looked like something bad had happened in them -- a kitchen fire or something -- but overall, it was like a different catastrophe happened up here.

Rushmore turned back to midtown and looked upon the vast expanse of Memorial Park, which spread out before him like a series of huge oases that broke up the center of midtown. The Saurian was in there somewhere. But where? Maybe, up here, there would be some clues. There were.

The trees of Memorial Park rustled too much; their largest branches waved wildly, as if the plant kingdom was somehow trying to get somebody's attention. Their green leaves made a rushing sound as they tangled and untangled against each other, many of them tearing off, while smaller branches cracked and split.

Rushmore could see the commotion was about a half-mile away. Intel on the Saurian was that he could track things by smell for at least twice that distance, though Rushmore wasn't certain if that meant keeping track of a pile of walking stone. He looked at the cityscape around the park and could see that there was a different kind of damage there, near the edge of the park. The sign of a rampage. Rushmore had seen it too many times before not to recognize it for what it was. He had hoped that maybe whatever set the Saurian off, it would manage to cool down in the time since then. Apparently, the chaos of the Omega Event prevented that.

Judging by the thrashing in the trees, the Saurian looked to be in the southern third of the park, between the park's lower boundary and the zoo. It suddenly occurred to him that in the last three days, he and his colleagues had been so busy trying to fix everything else that had gone wrong that nobody ever bothered to check on the animals.

Not like they'd blame us, Rushmore thought as he rotated his head to Thomas Jefferson and began heading down from the Highlands. The cliff here was pretty sheer, and at least one person fell to their death from it each year, even with heroes and citizen groups patrolling the edge. It was just a dangerous place. Probably not the best spot to build expensive housing. But then again, Rushmore noted to himself as he passed what had to be an eight-figure townhouse perched on the very edge of the cliffs, rich people do love to have things they're not supposed to have.

Rushmore knew his weight would break away any ledges his feet cold find purchase on, so he found an area that he didn't think would undercut a standing building, and jumped over the side, letting his hands and feet dig in the cliffside as he fell, gouging the earth, splitting the rock, and slowing his descent.

He could probably withstand a straight fall, but ever since his run-in with the Demolition Team, he was secretly concerned that he was only one hard shot from shattering into a million pebble-sized fragments, and whatever it was that made him intelligent and alive would escape and be lost forever.

He rode down the cliff face and jumped the last few feet, landing hard enough to make a small crater in the street. He landed with a loud boom, and he saw the rustling in the park suddenly cease. Great, he thought as he rotated his head to Teddy Roosevelt. I gave myself away.

No sense in setting myself up, Rushmore thought. He crouched down and leapt off the street, leaving behind another crater as the force of his takeoff buckled the ground below. He launched high into the air and arced over the blocks beneath as the park rushed up to meet him. Echelon protocol frowned on this, usually. The landings always left something to be desired. But right now, who was going to care? Half the city was in pieces anyway. For the first time, a guy like me doesn't have to worry about cracking the china, he thought with satisfaction as he came in for a landing.

Three tons of stone smashed through the park forest, tearing a great gouge in the earth. Rushmore came to a stop right before he plowed into Heritage Rock. Climbing out of the trench he'd dug with his landing, he patted the rock softly. Sorry to scare you, brother.

He listened for sounds of movement and heard nothing. Oh, damn, he thought. Saurian's gone into predator mode. I hate it when he does that.

Rushmore headed through the tree line to a nearby footpath, where he could walk across the park without smashing through the trees. Busting up a car or a building was regrettable, but that stuff was usually insured. A tree, now that takes time to grow. Besides, Rushmore thought, Baobab had this thing about regrowing old growth woodland. She felt we needed to live with the damage if we were ever going to learn something.

The Saurian felt close. "Hello!" Rushmore shouted out. "I know you're in here, man. You can see the forest shaking from the next area code. You want to come out, catch a steak or something?"

He listened for signs of life. Nothing.

"Saurian, this is Rushmore. Don't know if you've been watching the news, but the war's over. Everybody else is gone. It's just guys like you and me now. Why don't you come out so we can go open a few cold ones someplace safe?"

There was a burst of rustling leaves, then loud stomping. Rushmore could feel it through his feet.

"Oh, crap," he said, and he squared himself in the direction of the sound of the oncoming Saurian. He's been raging for three days straight. There was no telling how big and strong he'd gotten by now. If he's mad enough,

Rushmore thought, he'd be able to bite a pretty big chunk off of me without breaking a tooth.

The tree line exploded as a reptilian humanoid burst through it. It was rippling with muscles, covered with thick, plate-like scales. Its hands and arms were still proper humanoid size, but the creature was tucking them in to its body as it ran. There was a long, thick tail coming off its back, where there protruded a ridge of blunt dorsal spines. The head was a mass of bone and teeth, all carnivore. Its eyes had gotten yellow and beady, and the teeth had enlarged and distorted the jaw-line.

"Holy hell, man," Rushmore said. "You've really let yourself go."

The Saurian roared and leapt at Rushmore, its mouth open wide and its clawed, backward-bending legs held forward, like an enormous velociraptor. Rushmore reached forward to catch the monster before it made full contact. The idea was to absorb the impact of its charge and maybe throw it to one side, buy a few seconds of time.

The Saurian landed a lot harder than Rushmore expected, and the creature knocked the stone man backward, where it landed on his stomach and dug in. Its foot claws raked Rushmore's stone abdomen while it clamped its jaws down on his head and pounded away with its arms.

Rushmore could feel his head beginning to crack under the pressure from the Saurian's jaws. He rotated his head a full 360 degrees, twisting the Saurian's jaws and forcing it to let go. He followed up with a mighty left cross that caught the Saurian right on the side of its head, knocking it off and into the air. The Saurian crashed into a big tree, which half-uprooted under the weight of the impact. Both the Saurian and Rushmore took a second to get up, clear their heads, and start Round Two.

The Saurian stood and bowed a little, pushing its head forward and roaring. Rushmore grabbed a stone park bench and in a single movement, pulled it from the ground and hurled it into the Saurian's mouth. As the Saurian gagged and worked to wrest the bench out of its gullet, Rushmore moved in to finish the monster off with an uppercut. But the Saurian was too quick. It sidestepped and spun, slamming Rushmore with its tail and driving him into the ground.

Round Three. The Saurian was still roaring, but now it went in for another bite. Rushmore caught both the upper and lower jaw in his hands and wrestled with it for a second. Holding onto the mouth was proving difficult, and Rushmore didn't like the idea of getting one of his hands trapped in there.

"Screw this," Rushmore said, and he let go of the mouth, drove in with his shoulder and grappled the Saurian right under its head. He clasped his arms around the creature, twisted on his feet, and threw the Saurian to the ground, hanging on with all of his strength. He let the creature slip a little under his grip, but just enough to let him hitch his arms in tighter. He applied pressure right on the neck, and he could feel the Saurian reflexively swallow.

Just a minute or two now, Rushmore thought. He struggled to keep the pressure on the Saurian's neck without snapping it or putting him under too deeply, too quickly. The point was to bring the guy in, not mount his head on the wall.

He felt the Saurian's movements get slower and weaker, and after what felt like too long, he finally felt the creature's great mass sigh and relax. He let go and pushed the creature's bulky body off of him. It rolled onto the ground with a great thud.

Rushmore watched over the body, expecting it to transform back into something more human, more ordinary. But it did not. This was a first for the Saurian, though Rushmore had heard that ever since the Omega Event, Iron Will couldn't change back to his normal state, either. Maybe there was something out of whack with powers themselves. Maybe that was part of this whole thing; people's powers messing with the universe somehow.

He picked up the Saurian and heaved him over his shoulder for the long walk back to Echelon headquarters. He hoped the creature would stay unconscious until he could be placed into stasis. Having to subdue this guy twice in one day was asking a bit much, even from me, Rushmore thought.

I wonder why his power's gone out of whack, he thought. It's like it just sort of ran out, his ability to return to human. I wonder if that's what we all have to look forward to, our normality running out. Where would that leave me? I never had any to start with.

This made him think of Fluke once more, and how people had said that her luck had finally run out during the Spaghetti Bowl. That's what the media called the big highway fight, as if it was some kind of college football game. The whole thing enraged Rushmore; there were ordinary people up there who got hurt and died. This wasn't some game the gods played. There was a point to it all, and it wasn't for reporters to make snarky comments about while gunning for a Pulitzer.

Fluke died a few days after that. Word was she was thrown off the top of the Glenrock Tower. There were whispers that she was so distraught over that school bus that she killed herself, but that didn't seem like her. Besides, Praetorian was there. He got there just before she was pushed by the Doctrine, who was claiming revenge for some of the masks who went down during the Spaghetti Bowl throwdown.

The funeral was held in Bayside, and it was the biggest turnout of capes in Hudson City's history. There were also a few thousand demonstrators there who had had enough of masks and capes turning the city into a warzone. The group was led by parents of those schoolkids in the bus, but there were plenty more, too. The cops got involved, some young black mask decided to stir some trouble, and the next thing anybody knew, the whole thing turned into a riot that made the Spaghetti Bowl look like a jaywalking incident. Every mask with a grudge turned out to make a bad situation worse, and the capes on the scene had to respond. More masks got called in and the Bayside Riot was born. By the time it was over, there were dead, dying and missing on all sides. The civilians got it the worst. So did the cops, and the firefighters and EMTs on the scene. Anybody who got anywhere near Bayside that day got a taste of the chaos, and nobody walked out of it unaffected.

Rushmore thought of the riot and his part in it, battling more masks in one day than he ever thought he would. He thought of how he never got out of the cemetery; they just kept coming at him. At one point, there were at least half a dozen masks on him, and he stopped pulling his punches. He remembered seeing Skipjack lying dead on the ground and wondering if he was the one who did it. There were no other capes in the area, but he didn't remember putting the hurt on anybody who didn't look like they could take it.

Rushmore nearly quit afterwards. That was a year ago. Since then, a bunch of capes left the game, hung up their suits and just became civilians. Word was that a lot of black masks did the same; there was something about the Bayside thing that broke the rules. This was never supposed to be an open war between the capes and the masks. Whatever it was, it was about the civilians; one side protecting them, the other side threatening them. But for all of the doomsday plots and the hostage situations and all that, most masks never did the easy thing and killed civvies outright. Most of them didn't really have the stomach for it. There were a few, of course, but there could have been a lot more mass murder than there actually was. It was a different time, and a different kind of game.

After Bayside, a lot of new players entered on both sides. The rookie capes didn't have a problem with collateral damage, and the rookie masks didn't have the restraint of their elders. That's when the body count got out of hand. Echelon didn't know what to do. Nobody did. The Omega Event seemed to have fixed the problem before it got out of hand. Rushmore knew that one day, it would have. There would have been Bayside riots every month until the capes and the masks either killed each other off or all somehow left the game at the same time, and everybody knew that second option would never happen.

Rushmore reached the bridge to Echelon and felt the Saurian stirring. Got to hurry, he thought, and began running across to the island. Halfway across, the Saurian twitched and Rushmore knew he was out of time. He picked up speed, the great bulk of him and his prisoner slamming the bridge with more mass than it was really meant to hold. The bridge buckled at one point, just before Rushmore reached the island, but by then the Saurian had awoken, kicked and thrashed and twisted out of Rushmore's grasp.

He watched the Saurian fall into the river, diving deep beneath its surface and thrashing its tail for propulsion.

It was much faster submerged than Rushmore had thought it would be and within seconds, it was gone, under too much water to be seen anymore.

Rushmore searched the river's surface for a few minutes, hoping to catch some sign of the Saurian, but seeing none. He hoped that maybe it had gone into an even higher state of rage and would stand out of the water like a monster from those old Japanese movies. At least that way he would know where the bad guy was.

But there was nothing, and Rushmore walked slowly across the Echelon campus and back into the headquarters compound.

"Praetorian's gonna kill me," he said to himself.

A few hundred yards downstream, the Saurian emerged from the water. It clambered up the cliffs of the midtown shore, and once it had solid footing, it shook itself off like a dog. It looked back toward Rushmore.

Rushmore and the Saurian stared at each other over that long distance, and then the Saurian turned and walked back into the empty city. Whatever had enraged it, it was over now. The Saurian was still oversized and teratogenic, but it was calm.

Rushmore thought about chasing back into midtown to find the creature and bring it in. But he knew the look in the creature's eyes. It just wanted to be left alone.

"Good luck, buddy," Rushmore whispered. "Stay out of sight."

09
ASYLUM

Zlodic Viriskoya looked upon the battered skyline of midtown Hudson City and wondered why it was that he was still around to enjoy the view. Moments earlier, he had powered off the computer screens in his study that linked into satellite feeds directly above the metropolis. The satellites had come at no small cost, but thankfully Korovia's small, efficient and extremely advanced space flight program was able to place a global network in about half a year, and at a cost most other countries would pay to get a passable cellular telephone network up and running. Known as Highlord, the network offered Zlodic the opportunity to grab minutely detailed video feed, through any number of advanced optical enhancements, anywhere in the world. Usually, he used it to obtain critical intelligence on a rival, a party worthy of his revenge, or on the movements of the Echelon heroes who had appointed themselves the UN's superpowered hatchet men. Today, he was using it merely to see if there was anybody at all on the streets of Hudson City, or any other major urban area on the planet. He had set Highlord to key in on any movement of objects with a mass of more than 50 kilos, but aside from finding some deer and falling wreckage - which Highlord automatically discounted - there was nothing. And why not? Ever since the sky blinked out for that terrifying split-second three days before, the world had been empty of people.

Well, not entirely empty, Zlodic thought as he looked over his shoulder and watched a beautiful, light-haired clone approach him. She was one of the consort models he had been fine-tuning for mass production in the Asian sex markets, but for now, she was merely a much-enjoyed prototype. I must remind myself to make her a friend, Zlodic thought. Perhaps a brunette. One that reminds me of that farm girl from Vladistoya. She was...special.

The consort approached and laid her hands lightly on Zlodic's shoulders. He was already dressed, even though it was only a few minutes after dawn. Rather than the usual business suit, he had opted for hunting clothes, casual but presentable, comfortable but serious, functional but stylish.

"My lord does not sleep?" the consort said. "Perhaps he would prefer some company."

She leaned over and kissed him softly on the neck. Zlodic liked what he felt, but it did not arouse him as it ought to have. He gently waved her off. "I am preoccupied," he said.

The consort instantly backed off and took a different posture and tone -- one of genuine concern, and of loving interest. "With what?"

"There are no people left, Calliope," Zlodic said. Talking to her was like talking to himself, except he could not always anticipate what she would say in return. That made things feel somewhat better. Less lonely, and yet, not really. The Korovian compound was fully staffed with more than 150 clones from a dozen different templates, most of them genetically optimized to have slight variations within their genoform that kept them all from looking like animated escapees from a mannequin factory.

"There is you, my lord," Calliope said. "And does not that matter above all?"

"It does," Zlodic said, looking out over the balcony of his study. "It does," he added quietly.

Calliope cocked her head a little and studied her creator. "Why do you not make me believe you?"

Zlodic gripped the balcony rail. "Because everything I have striven for suddenly means nothing," he said. "The Regent was to break an already broken world and forge it into something new. Something beautiful. Something better."

"And is now not your chance?" said Calliope. She gestured to the still skyline. "This city is yours to take, if you wish. As is any other portion of the world you could desire. All that stands in your way are the heroes of Echelon. Have you not defeated them before?"

Zlodic thought of the six times he had the Praetorian subdued and at his mercy, and how every time, some tiny overlooked detail would ruin it, provide his nemesis with the opportunity to escape, turn the tables. It was only after the sixth time that Zlodic was finally honest enough with himself to admit what he knew all along: he was the smartest man on the planet, by a goodly margin. He had an eidetic memory so vast that to print out the information it stored would create a paper trail to Jupiter and back. He figured that out once, while awaiting trial.

His problem was not that he was not smart enough to foil those standing between him and the rest of the world. The problem was that he let them win, every time. He could not help himself. After all, as much as he hated the Praetorian and his many allies great and small, they were that which made him feel a part of something. Being the Regent was more than running the world's smallest - and richest - country, being the UN's most hated head of state, and being the world's very public enemy number one. But being the one man the Praetorian feared...that was something else. What would there be, if that was gone? Indeed, there was a world to remake, entire populations to decimate with genetically targeted nanoviruses, weather patterns to restore, ecosystems to rebuild, and a new breed of humanity to carefully, oh, so carefully reintroduce to a world that had suffered so much at the hands of people already. Once that was done, what else would there be? To sit back, content, knowing he had won? Watching the world he had made slowly grow older before him?

The thought scared him worse than anything, for it would mean that he was well and truly alone.

"There must be somebody," Zlodic said.

"What was that?" Calliope said.

Zlodic shook his head. "Nothing. Just a thought."

"It is more than that," Calliope said, tracing her fingers through his hair and tucking a lock behind his ear. "You are on the verge of something. I can hear it in your voice."

Zlodic looked at her. This was an unusual amount of insight for a clone. "Hear it?"

Calliope smiled shyly, caught off guard. "Yes," she said, blushing. "I can tell what you are feeling even when you do not."

"You were built for it," Zlodic said.

"No," Calliope answered, hurt. "It is because I love you," she said before she turned and left his study.

Zlodic watched her go, not knowing what to think. Love? Impossible. I did not program her to feel it. Surely she is mimicking something she has picked up elsewhere, some subtle combination of verbal and facial cues, body language...

He thought of his tea service with Sigma, the day of the Event, how they held hands, and how afterwards, they said nothing, merely standing there in tense silence, not knowing what to say, but wanting to find out. He remembered watching Sigma leave without saying goodbye or even looking at him, and for the first time, he found it impossible to tell someone they could not leave.

He did not know which vexed him more. The moment between himself and Sigma, or the degree to which Calliope picked up on it, even though she was not even in the room at the time. This bears study, Zlodic told himself. But not right now. She was right. I am on the verge of something. Time to discover what it is.

He returned to his study table, a massive piece of imperial furniture carved from a single block of ancient Amazonian hardwood and embedded with tiny, virtually invisible holoprojectors. As Zlodic sat at the table, proximity sensors powered up the computer and a projected touchscreen with many different panes to it shimmered into view, hovering before him.

Zlodic moved some of the panes around to make room for a database screen and the satellite feed from Highlord. He checked the morning sweeps and found nothing; still no people anywhere, except for the various costumed gladiators who made Hudson their battleground. With some disdain, Zlodic noted the rosters of individuals catalogued and marked by Highlord. The heroes were only too familiar to him: Praetorian. Sigma. Rushmore. Iron Will. Fast Forward. A list of other names who could only have been newcomers to the Echelon training program. A police academy for tomorrow's caped heroes, Zlodic thought. What a cruel joke.

The list of super-criminals and most wanted was almost as familiar. Most were figures he had contracted some work through at one time or another, or who he might have manipulated into combat with the Echelon to serve a distantly related purpose. Some were independent operators. And some were truly dangerous. Their list was as long as the heroes', who were doubtlessly chasing them across Hudson right now, bent on putting them in the Echelon lockdown until they confess to the world's greatest unsolvable crime.

The Saurian remains free, Zlodic noticed. How does one not manage to catch a half-man, half-dinosaur on a rampage? Dreamweaver, the Underling, Horde, someone with Skipjack's energy signature but not Skipjack himself -- a son, perhaps? -- and Threshold were the ones that merited the most attention. The rest are as inconsequential as Echelon's trench diggers, Zlodic thought. Even the gods have an underclass, it seems.

He sat back and looked at the names. These were the only survivors of the Omega Event. Or perhaps not survivors, he corrected himself, but those who remained afterward. It remained to be seen what the Omega Event really was. Phased time distortion, mass hallucination, parallel dimensional bubble and three space-time complications Zlodic himself had discovered but not yet bothered to name could all have yielded the same result.

But which one? Perhaps none of them. It could always be as simple as the people of the world were instantly obliterated by a massive energy pulse that unraveled the quantum signatures that unified every single member of homo sapiens.

Signatures. Quantums. Species. That's it, he thought.

He cross-referenced each hero and villain Highlord had detected against the global database of Echelon signatures, the UN standard system for determining those who were merely extraordinary humans, and those who were something more. Something...super.

Anything below E20 was considered human. This mattered to the UN, which quite openly feared that were the number of superhumans on the planet to increase substantially, there might emerge an entirely separate species of humanity, one that could fly, deflect bullets, project fire and control minds. One that was trapped in a civil war of its own, with one side obsessed with serving a humanity that did not deserve it, and the other obsessed with serving only itself, even to the point of detriment. Of all of the problems this world faced, Zlodic thought, we were its worst. Its most pernicious. Its most unsolvable. Until somebody solved it. If I could only discern how.

Zlodic looked at the list and arranged the entries by Echelon rating. Most of the familiar names were within ten points of each other, somewhere in the 40s or 50s. There were a few, like Threshold and Rushmore, who stood out in the 70s and 80s. Praetorian was off the chart, as was Voyager, although she went missing before the Echelon ratings were instituted, so her power level could only be guessed at. Made little difference, Zlodic thought. She is gone ten years now, out into space, over to the great hereafter, or down some rabbit hole a villain contrived for her. One who needs these heroes much less than I do, apparently. I would have let her go, if only to watch her work. Her archival footage is amazing.

Zlodic looked at his own rating. E-21. Just barely super. In on a technicality.

Just seeing it made him angry. I am more than human, and yet I cannot fathom why. The genetic programs his fathers and mothers had engineered did remarkable things with his personal helixes, combining more genetic information into a single strand than there was supposed to be room for. It was what made him able to compete with Olympic athletes without training, what made him age at one sixth the normal rate, what made him immune to disease, and what made him smart enough to dwarf the world's greatest minds with the sheer scope of his intellect.

I am the future of mankind, Zlodic told himself. The world's future is my destiny. And yet, there is so little that is special about me compared to these others. Invincibility. Energy manipulation. Duplication. The gods have their underclass, indeed.

He cast the thoughts from his mind. After all, Sigma was merely E-24, and she was the one people suggested was the real power behind Praetorian. The one who could see the things for which the world's mightiest man would be needed. The one from whom no villain could hide his or her intentions. The one with the backstage view of the universe's infinite clockwork, and who knew what time it was even before it had ticked over.

"What matters," he said, "is the difference between 19 and 20." What was it that preserved superhumans from the Omega Event? And more than that, what was it that preserved these particular supers? At last count, there was about one E-20+ for every 100,000 regular people. Most of them did not even know they had powers lurking within them. Most of them lived lives as normal as their fellows around them, completely ignorant to the collective destiny to which they were heirs. But their power level was not enough to save them. What was it?

What was it?

What? Was? It?

He seethed, so unable to find the answer to such a simple question. Part of it was the variables; he could go into a trance and crunch through every genetic variation of everybody on that list, but he was sure that Praetorian would try to pay him a visit between now and then, and it never paid to get visited by the Praetorian when one is more asleep than awake.

Besides, what would it matter? Nobody knows more about genetic micro-variations than I do, he thought. I practically invented them, and there is not enough difference at the quantum level to make some people resonant and others non-harmonic. It's just impossible.

Unless somebody invented a new form of energy, that is. Somebody who lucked into it, somebody who kept it quiet, somebody who did not need the world to know what he or she did.

Some amateur.

Zlodic pounded the desk so hard his holoscreens shimmered. Dammit! It should have been one of us who did this! It should have been me! Haven't I earned at least as much? Haven't I primed the world for its fall? Haven't I set all the blocks into motion? And for what? All so some make-believe mad scientist can take everything I have done and put the final finishing touch on it and know that he was the one for whom the world trembled.

Damn you, whoever you are. Damn you to hell.

No, Zlodic thought as he closed the Echelon database, leaving a sat image of the emptiness of Hudson over his desktop. Damn you elsewhere. Hell is here, he thought. And it is mine.

Just then, the holoscreens all pulsed red and a soft tone went off, alerting Zlodic that there was movement on the streets nearby. Zlodic pulled himself close to the desk and hit the Highlord feed, auto-zooming in on four figures, one person chased by three, all about a block and a half from the Korovian compound. Zlodic looked at it for a few seconds before confirming what he'd instantly suspected. Whoever they are, they're coming here.

He pinpointed each figure and cross-referenced it against the Echelon database to instantly gain their identities. The runner was a thief known as Scrounge. Elasticity powers, plus the ability to adhere to things. Sticky fingers, indeed. He was pursued by three Echelon-sanctioned capes: Icarus, the Redeemer and Section 8.

Zlodic frowned. Scrounge was a known entity; he frequently contracted his services to the highest bidder when he wasn't taking down scores himself, often taking extreme risks to steal things he didn't truly need. But the three heroes after him had minimal files; more fresh recruits from Echelon, there was no telling how reasonable or restrained they might be. Probably not much of either, Zlodic thought.

He touched an invisible button on the surface of his desk that activated his perimeter nanodefenses. Across the compound, a cloud of specially targeted nanobots would release, each specifically targeting the genetic sequences of the three heroes. He looked at his store of nano and fretted over the small amount left. He had depended on a fresh supply of Korovium to replenish his nanofoundry, located in the sub-levels of the manor house. Now it was almost empty, and his failsafe defense against invading supers had only one or two shots left.

Zlodic headed toward the manor house's front doors, and was joined by a muscular male clone along the way. "Sire, security teams are standing by."

"Thank you, Gunnar, but I don't think that will be necessary," Zlodic said without looking at him. "Just the same, if things do get uncivilized out there, do try to only wound our intruders."

"Understood," Gunnar said with a nod. "Let us hope we can resolve this peacefully."

"We'll see," Zlodic said. "The day is still young."

Gunnar ran down a wide hallway that took him into the depths of the house. His location was irrelevant, as he was already in what amounted to telepathic contact with the rest of the security detail. All were of a recent template Zlodic had designed with such radical advancement to a portion of their brains that they could actually hear and transmit radio waves. None had lived very long, however, as they were also prone to getting brain cancer. An unfortunate glitch, that.

Zlodic walked out of the manor house and to the front gate of the compound. Security clones dressed in armored battlesuits and carrying lasers held their positions within the walls; the view to the outside fed directly to their helmets by floating midge cameras that hovered high above the compound itself. They could have patched into the Highlord feed, but it ate up too much memory in their suit computers.

The gates opened, and a man appeared, wearing a strange outfit that resembled a stylized commando suit with numerous pouches and pockets, except for the arms and legs. Scrounge.

He was running full tilt toward the compound, and behind him, Zlodic could see the three pursuers; one an athletic man flying low to the ground with a pair of large angelic wings, the second a large and muscular individual wearing a full-body suit made of dark leather with a heavy cape enshrouding him, the third a scabrous monstrosity of a man wearing what appeared to be an athletic mask and a stylized straitjacket that did nothing to impede his movement. Icarus. The Redeemer. Section 8.

Scrounge seemed to know where his chasers were. Right as the Redeemer fired a volley of flechettes from a set of launchers in his gauntlets, Scrounge shot his arm out, which stretched like rubber and smacked into the top column of the Korovian gate, sticking to it. Scrounge leapt upwards and let his arm snap back into shape as he shot out his other arm, attached it to a gatehouse within the compound, and pulled himself toward it. It was like watching a gibbon brachiate with long frog's tongues instead of arms.

Zlodic stood casually at the entrance of the compound, with his hands behind his back. The security team tensed, awaiting the order to fire once their master was run over by the incoming heroes, but they got no such order.

Icarus flapped his wings hard and braked, landing on his feet and folding his wings behind him. The Redeemer skidded to a stop, his cape flaring out dramatically and the eyes of his distinctive cowl offering a dull yellow glow. Section 8 stopped short, grabbing onto the Redeemer's solid frame and digging his feet in.

"Gentlemen," Zlodic said.

"You are harboring a known criminal," Icarus said. "We have orders from the Praetorian to bring him in."

"For what, might I ask?" Zlodic said. "Surely whatever he has stolen this time cannot be more important than the disappearance of the human race."

The Redeemer took a step forward. "Give him over, Regent. Don't do something you're going to regret." The Redeemer's voice seemed to buzz in Zlodic's skull, making his brain fire in ways it was not supposed to.

Zlodic stared into the Redeemer's yellow eyes. "Don't bother using that voice of yours on me," he said. "It may work on those underworld minions you so love to terrify, but I am not one of those. Frankly, I find it insulting that you even tried."

Section 8 laughed nervously and thrashed his arms. "Don't you freaky deak on us, man! Don't you freaky deak!"

Zlodic regarded him as he would an untrained dog. He returned his attentions to Icarus, who seemed to be the leader of the bunch.

"The man you chased here is under the diplomatic protection of the Republic of Korovia," Zlodic said. "As Regent of Korovia, I hereby grant him full diplomatic immunity. Kindly tell the Praetorian that even now, UN laws and standards must still apply, and I expect him to continue upholding them."

The Redeemer tensed. "This is ridiculous. We're taking him," he said, stepping forward. Zlodic held up one hand, which stopped him.

"Before you continue, do you know what I will do if you set a single finger upon me, or enter my compound?"

The heroes said nothing.

"I will utter the command word that will activate all of the nanoagents you have all breathed in. I can assure you, the effects will be most unpleasant."

Section 8 looked up at the sky and swatted at invisible bugs, his way of getting the nano off of him.

The Redeemer pointed at Zlodic. "You cannot hide in here forever, tyrant. We will return, and when we do, your days are over."

"We shall see," Zlodic said menacingly. "Until then, I will be sure to prepare for you specifically, Mr. Needham."

The Redeemer looked sharply at Zlodic. What did he say? How did he know my real name?

"I know everything," Zlodic said with some satisfaction. "Which is why I know how to defeat each and every one of you. Now leave me before I find myself needing to prove it."

Icarus extended his wings and glared at Zlodic before addressing his colleagues. "Come on. Let's go."

He lifted off the ground and glided slowly as the Redeemer and Section 8 turned from the Korovian compound and headed back across the city toward Echelon headquarters. Zlodic did not close the gates until he saw that all three figures were well out of sight.

He exhaled slowly, and then sought Scrounge, who was being held by the security detail in a discreet guardhouse away from the gate.

Scrounge stood when Zlodic entered and held his hands out. "Regent, man, thank you so much for letting me in. I thought those guys were going to kill me."

"Perhaps I should have let them," Zlodic said. "What made you think you could come here, to my home, to seek sanctuary? What made you think you were welcome? What made you think you had the right?" With each new sentence, Zlodic's voice grew a fraction louder and more intense, and Scrounge shrunk from him, suddenly unsure if hiding in Korovia was a better option than simply surrendering to Echelon's newest agents.

"I'm sorry, Regent," Scrounge said. "I didn't know where else to go. I can't handle this city being as empty as it is. I just...I just..." He looked distraught. "I knew there were some people here, you know?"

Zlodic nodded and placed a hand on Scrounge's shoulder. "I do," he said softly.

Scrounge relaxed.

"So tell me," Zlodic said, sitting down across from Scrounge and dismissing the security guards, "what was worth incurring the wrath of Echelon?"

Scrounge smiled, opened one of the larger zippered pockets on his utility vest, and produced a diamond the size of a fist. It was perfectly smooth and oblong, the shape of a dinosaur's egg, with a starburst of blue within the middle of it. The Star of Atlantis. The only gemstone of its kind in the world.

Zlodic motioned to the stone with a silent "May I?" that the Scrounge accepted. He handed over the Star. Zlodic held it in his hand and grinned.

"It is heavier than I thought it would be," he said.

"I know!" Scrounge said with a tone of surprise. "I always knew it weighed more than regular ice, but this thing is just heavy."

"I must ask, what did you plan on doing with it?" Zlodic said, handing it back.

Scrounge held it and looked at it, almost like he suddenly did not know what it was. "Hell if I know," he said. "The security was always impossible to crack on this thing. I just figured without anybody around, I could just bully through the sensors and take it. So I did."

"And what if those caped heroes had caught you? What then? Would it have been worth it?"

"Probably not," Scrounge said. "I gotta be honest with you, man. I don't think I can do this anymore. Stealing stuff, I mean."

"Reforming your wayward habits, then?" Zlodic said.

Scrounge shook his head. "Nah, it's not like that. I mean...half the stuff I take, it's just for the challenge of it, you know? Now, it's not even hard. I mean, I've got about $100 million in gold I lifted from the Federal Reserve over the last three days just because I was looking for something to do. Even if things do go back to normal, you think I'm going to try to smelt that stuff and sell it? Hell no, man."

"You strike me as one of those lawbreakers who wants to get caught," Zlodic said. "Seems like a terrible waste of your particular talents."

"Look, I'm not gonna lie...I kind of liked that those capes came after me when I hit the museum because it let me know that I wasn't the last guy on Earth. I was starting to get worried about that. But I'm not looking to get busted back to lockup, either. I'm never going back, man." He grew serious. "I am never going back."

"Then why take the risk?" Zlodic said.

"I don't know...same reason why you keep daring the Praetorian, I guess. We've all got our reasons." He paused and thought on it some more. "I like it when people say I can't go somewhere or I can't take something. It gives me a reason to figure out how to prove them wrong."

Zlodic tapped his chin. "I can see why you might find things a bit dull, then."

Scrounge exhaled and made a dismissive wave of his hand. "'Dull' is not the word for it. It's like somebody just called the entire game on account of the rain, you know? Without people in it, this city is just one big treasure chest that's wide open to a guy like me. Even if every cape from Echelon was out patrolling, they still couldn't possibly keep everything worth stealing in this damned town safe. And I should be happy; I should be taking everything I can, while I can. And for a while, I did."

He looked at the floor.

"I dreamed about this. A day when there were no more citizens, no more cops, no more capes, just a world full of scores for me to take," Scrounge said. "And now I've got it, and only three days later, I'm bored."

"Perhaps you simply have a short attention span," Zlodic said. "Or a lack of ambition." How might he respond to this, Zlodic thought.

Scrounge looked at Zlodic. "Whatever, man. I don't think these people are coming back."

Zlodic thought about what he said.

"In fact, I know they aren't. I can feel it in my gut. And my gut never lies."

He placed the Star on an empty chair next to him. "You know, I don't even want this thing anymore. I don't want any of it. I...don't know what I want."

Zlodic looked at the Star, sitting discarded. He thought of the endless satellite feeds he had reviewed since the world went empty, how many times he had imagined the overwriting of the human race, the utter Korovian domination over all other nations and regimes. He thought of all who would oppose him, and what his victory would mean to his defeated rivals. He thought of what Scrounge had just said as well, about nobody coming back. All of it, gone. All of it meaningless.

He had spent hours upon hours trying to discern the science behind the Omega Event and when things might return to normal, but he knew, as well as Scrounge did, that there was no normal to go back to. This was it. This was the new normal, forevermore. "I know what you mean," he said to Scrounge, and extended his hand to him. "Welcome to my home. My name is Zlodic."

Scrounge took off his goggles and his gloves and shook Zlodic's hand. "Harry. Harry Gleason. Pleased to meet you."

"So tell me, Harry, would you be interested in a little project I have in mind?" Zlodic said.

Harry shrugged. "Sure, man, whatever you want. I'm up for anything."

"Good," Zlodic said. "Then come with me. We have a great deal of work to do."

10
DUMB LUCK

Simon flew through the heart of a thunderstorm, letting the concussion of the thunder and the energy of the lightning batter his body. He liked the feel of the storm's fury, though none of it harmed him any more than a soft breeze might. Still, there was something primal about it, something that made him feel closer to his unique destiny than almost anything else did. It was majestic. It was also something he had never shared with anyone else. Not his team mates, with whom he so rarely actually worked anyway. Most of them would merely slow him down, and would expose themselves to excessive dangers, considering the kinds of threats he took on. And the storm passages were never the sort of detail he gave over to the media when they conducted their interviews of him, when the long-form journalists wrote their features on him, when the bloggers tried to scoop the world with some little detail about the world's mightiest man that nobody had managed to land.

It was the sort of thing that let him feel alone, apart from a world that constantly needed him, constantly called to him, constantly asked for more.

And now, it was a world gone quiet.

He emerged from the storm clouds and was still a few hundred miles from the coast of France, by his estimation. Flying low over the water like this took more time; it would have been much more efficient to simply orbit low, point down at his destination and descend, but this way gave him time to think.

So far, the day had been a bust. He had overflown every major metropolis on the Eastern seaboard once again, this time looking specifically for any signs of E-level activity. He knew the world was empty; he had given up trying to find any pockets of people who had been spared by what Ellen was now calling the Omega Event. All he knew was that a handful of capes and masks were still around, which meant there might be others elsewhere.

He knew the numbers. There was about one person in a million with Echelon energy levels over 20, indicating the kinds of abilities that might be considered super powers. The entire Echelon rating system seemed to be based on arbitrary science, Simon thought, in no small part because it was a power scale that could not rate him on it. What use is there if it cannot provide a context for those like me?

Six billion people. One in a million with powers. That made a world population of about 6,000 people who had abilities far beyond those of their normal mortal counterparts. These people all filled in the Echelon scale fairly evenly, making an equal distribution in power levels. Strangely, those who became masks and those who became capes always seemed to be roughly equal to each other, as if some invisible hand had ensured that no one side had more strength than the other.

They never had their Praetorian, he thought. How many of them did I count as? A hundred? A thousand? Maybe more.

He flew over the Channel Islands, slowing down just a bit to scan for any signs of the nobleman adventurer who simply called himself the Seigneur. Once he knew what energy wavelengths signified Echelon levels--that is, once Ellen explained it to him--Simon became the one tasked with finding out which capes and masks outside of Hudson City had made it through the Event. So far, the results were pretty grim. Could it be that there was something about Hudson City that offered its supers a greater chance to remain behind? Perhaps.

Maybe there was something about the people left behind that spoke to their qualities, Simon thought. It was a struggle at all times not to allow his sense of unique ability lead to a feeling of entitlement or superiority. It was especially hard to think otherwise, now. Something hit the world all at once, and only a few of us were strong enough to survive it, Simon thought. Only a few of us were fit enough to inherit the world.

He zoomed over Jersey, over Guernsey, even over little Sark looking for the Seigneur, but he wasn't there. Even if he was, Simon doubted he would be interested in coming back to Hudson with him. That one had been content to be the world's only super-powered nobleman, governing a tiny island whose people thought it a privilege to live in both Europe's last remaining feudal fiefdom as well as in one of two sovereign territories ruled by a super. The other was Korovia.

The French countryside was beautiful, as always, and in a short time, Simon was in Paris, looking, scanning and losing hope. The City of Lights was as empty as everywhere else. None of the nationally sanctioned heroes were here. Neither could the numerous villains who stood to oppose them be found. Nothing. Somehow, Simon thought at least a few of the French heroes would remain, as if their unwillingness to bow to anybody's standards would also make them proof against the Omega Event.

Brussels, London and Copenhagen were the same. Helsinki, Berlin, Moscow, Prague, too. When he hit Geneva on the long way back, he picked something up. This was not unexpected. There was something about this city that always brought out the interesting ones.

He touched down near the city's signature spouting fountain, and was relieved to see that it was still running. The Artifex had said that most of the automated things in the world could be counted on to keep going for some time, but without regular maintenance, one by one, they would all fail. But for now, it was nice to see that the vast majority of them were still going. Despite the widespread damage done to so many cities in the first minutes after the Event, the world still seemed like it was merely waiting for its people to return.

Simon homed in on the power reading he'd picked up and found a grim-looking avenger sitting in an open-air cafe, wearing his combat costume, having a cup of tea and some light cake. He noticed Simon approaching and waved him over.

"Ah, Praetorian!" he said. "Nice to see a friend. Won't you have some tea with me?"

Simon recognized him at once. The was The Loner, one of those dark-hearted revenge types whose powers were never clearly defined by anybody, and who seemed to get by more on his reputation than anything he actually did. It scared the hell out of the masks, which was good, but Simon had a hard time trusting it. People who wear a cape need to make the world know why they do it, he thought. And capes who act like masks raise difficult questions with no easy answers.

"I trust you paid for that," Simon said, gesturing to the food.

The Loner gestured with his hands, suggesting what Simon said was ridiculous. "But of course! Just because the storekeeps are away does not give me the right to steal from them."

Simon noticed that indeed, there were a few euro coins on the table. I'll be damned, Simon thought. He really had planned to pay.

"So tell me, what brings you to Geneva?"

"I was about to ask you the same question," Simon said. "I thought your beat was...not here."

The Loner wagged a finger at Simon. "Ah, Praetorian, my beat, as you say, is all over the world. Wherever there is crime, there is also the Loner."

"Right," Simon said as he pulled out a chair and sat down. "Who were you after in Geneva?"

"The Regent, actually. I was doing some research with a few of my contacts in the UN legal community. They have been working on a long-term project to get around the loopholes Korovia has been abusing."

"The Regent," Simon said. "He makes a mockery of everything we stand for."

The Loner sipped his tea, and as he did, Simon realized that this must be why so many masks and capes eschewed those full-facial models any more. Impossible to catch a coffee break with them on. And if you're protecting an identity, it didn't pay to unmask at your local barista.

"Indeed he does," the Loner said. His accent seemed French when the conversation started, but very gradually, it was shifting to German. "This is why I was called here. I had evidence on some arms trafficking exploits in Africa that the Legal sections needed. I was, of course, only too glad to hand it over. That was three days ago."

Simon knew what he meant. That was when everybody went away.

"You know, Praetorian, in the fifteen years I have worn this mask, I have experienced three global events of the kind men like you and I would find of special interest. The first was the Hong Kong incident in 1989, right after Tiananmen Square. Do you remember that?"

Simon nodded. "I do," he said. "Sometimes I wish I could forget it."

"Don't we all," the Loner said. "The second was Antarctica, 1996. Dreamweaver came this close to having us all believe we were under alien attack."

Simon nodded again. "Perhaps the greatest bait and switch in the history of mankind. There was almost a nuclear war over that one."

"Yes," the Loner said again, and sipped more tea. "And now, this. I had hoped you might tell me what is going on."

"I don't know," Simon said.

The Loner placed his teacup on the table and looked at Simon evenly. "I do not like it when you lie to me."

"I'm not lying," Simon said. But he knew that he was.

"You know something that you will not share," the Loner said. "That was always your problem. Not just you, but all of the capes like you. You keep things to yourself, you have your own agendas, you create divisions where there should be none. And then you wonder why the Loner is as he is."

Simon tried to find something to say that would defuse things. The situation was more complex than the Loner would have it; there were things he did not understand, considerations he had not taken into account.

"Interesting," the Loner said, nodding with his chin toward some point over Simon's shoulder. "It appears that we have company."

Simon turned to see who it was, but there was nobody there. When he turned back, the Loner was gone.

Simon sat in his chair. Dammit, he thought. He did it again. And now there's no way in hell he's coming back to Hudson with me until he feels like it. Good going, Simon. First E-level you find since the Event and he pulls a dine and dash on you. Smart.

"You look sad, Simon," he heard a female say to him. The voice was familiar, and it made Simon jump when he heard it.

A beautiful woman in a skintight tactical suit pulled out the Loner's chair and sat down. She had fair skin and a mass of reddish hair in tight curls that spilled over her shoulders. Her outfit was colored in subtle shades of metallic green and gold and somehow reflected the colors in her eyes. Jennifer Ireland. Also known as Fluke.

"Jennifer!" Simon said. "Jenny...Jen." His voice grew more composed and formal with each different name.

Jen smiled at Simon, and his stomach felt like it fell out of him. "You can call me whatever you want, soldier boy. You know that," she said.

"I can't call you anything," Simon said. "You're dead, and I know that, and you're just a figment of my imagination."

Jen squinted at Simon like he had played a joke on her. "Really, Simon? That's all you have to say to me after everything we went through? Come on...I know you can do better than that."

"I don't have time for this," Simon said, and he shoved his chair back from the table. "I am needed elsewhere."

"Of course you are," Jen said, still seated. She did not seem perturbed at his tone or that he was leaving. "But you need to know that you don't get to leave me just like that. Not after how we left things."

"We didn't leave anything," Simon said. "You made that perfectly clear."

"We all make mistakes, Simon," Jen said. "And we all have to live with them."

"You didn't," Simon said bitterly before he took off, blasting into the sky so fast that he broke the sound barrier only a hundred feet or so above the cafe, rattling the windows at street level. It was the kind of move he never pulled in civilized areas, because it frightened people. But he had to admit to himself that right now, it felt really good.

He went over England one last time, scanning at high speed, fairly certain that any readings he did pick up would only force him to double back and search again. At this speed, he'd be miles away before he could fix the position. He found nothing as he crossed the middle of

Britain, and saw no major movement on the ground, save for the migration of some flocks of sheep.

He headed northwest, over the water to Iceland. There was only one super here, and even that was an aberration. In a country of 300,000 people, the odds were against any of them having significant E-levels. But one did. Too bad he became a mask, Simon thought. Ragnarok tended to operate away from home -- better hunting elsewhere -- but there was word that he had given up the villain thing, at least for a while. Woman troubles. Other intel, just as questionable, was that he'd experienced a death in the family. Either way, he had supposedly gone back to the home country to collect his thoughts. If that was true, then he'd be sitting in the depths of one of the volcanos, where the magma could not hurt him and where the rest of the world was guaranteed to leave him alone.

Good thing I'm not the rest of the world, Simon thought with some satisfaction as he picked up a spike in Echelon energy about 50 miles outside of Reykjavik. Time to pay Ragnarok a visit.

He flew to the mouth of one of the island's many active lava spouts and dove in, knowing his cape would burn off, but that the rest of his outfit would survive the plunge. Funny how whatever protected his body protected his close clothing as well. It seemed to work like that for anybody who could shrug off damage to any appreciable degree.

The world went bright red as Simon plunged through the churning lava, and there, in its fiery depths, was Ragnarok, floating in the liquid fire, dressed like an ancient Viking warlord, a man dedicated to embodying the Nordic apocalypse after which he had been named. Simon recalled his battles with him, how they were always long, extended affairs that seemed to leave whatever area in which they fought in ruins. There could be no confronting this one without there being extensive collateral damage; the shockwaves Ragnarok put out every time he hit something made him a walking disaster zone.

Simon could feel the heat of the lava on him as if he was out in direct sun for too long; maybe he'd have a light residual burn once he left, but in a few minutes it would heal itself. Just the same, it made him unwilling to open his mouth to speak. Swallowing lava: not a good idea.

He moved to Ragnarok and touched him on the shoulder. His costume was actually a set of oversized armor, plates upon plates, all adorned with the ancient runes of his forefathers. Somewhere in there was the man, under his huge horned helmet with its brooding faceplate. His eyes must have been closed, for the eye slits were dark, shadowed. Simon knew from his own experience that Ragnarok's eyes blazed brightly. Even here, it would have been noticeable.

Simon grabbed him by a shoulder guard and shook him. Wake up! He did it again, but Ragnarok was unresponsive. He didn't move as if unconscious or dead; there was enough resistance to tell Simon that somebody was home. But there was no reaction more meaningful than that. No response. No interest in anything but the solace of fire.

Stay out of trouble, Simon thought at Ragnarok as he let him go. I wonder if he even knows, he thought, as he flew upward and to the bubbling, spurting surface.

He splashed free from the lava and flew into the ocean, so the burning rock that still clung to him could instantly cool, darken and crack off. When he was finally free of the last few pieces, he left the ocean and headed back across the Atlantic, toward home. He put on some speed and was instantly blown dry.

He thought of Fluke, back in Geneva. It wasn't the first time he'd seen her, but he was beginning to fear that it would not be the last, either. Since the Event, he could have sworn he spotted her in the corner of his eye, there, watching him only to disappear the moment he tried focusing on her. For a remnant of my memory or an expression of my guilt, she's awfully willful, he thought.

Rather than go straight to Hudson, Simon veered north a little so that he could pay Toronto a visit. The number of supers there had grown a bit in recent years, and there was a Canadian concentration analogous to the unusually high numbers in Hudson. Maybe there would be a find, one who wouldn't mind a lift back to Echelon.

He came into Toronto's airspace low and slow, out of respect for the city's request that people like him didn't boom the locals. Ever since Airstrike terrorized the city, they were all a bit jumpy about anybody who could fly under their own power.

Simon scanned the urban expanse and found two signatures right on top of each other. "Better take a look," he said to himself, and sped toward them.

On the outskirts of the city, he found Rolling Thunder grappling with Rat Bastard. It seemed like a mismatch, since Rolling Thunder could call down lightning bolts at will and blow around his opponents with gusts of controlled air. But Rat Bastard had him covered with a hundred angry rats, mice and other biting vermin, and it was only the most focused of minds that could ignore such a horrifying assault.

Rolling Thunder called lightning upon himself, which electrocuted the creatures on him. They all fell away from him, dead and smoking. He was covered with bite and scratch wounds, and had blood all over him. He's going to need a shot, Simon thought.

Rat Bastard bared his claws, hissed and crouched, ready to leap at Rolling Thunder, but Simon intervened and grabbed him by the throat, holding him off the ground and at a safe distance. Rat Bastard screeched and clawed and kicked at Simon, but it did nothing to him.

"You alright?" Simon asked Rolling Thunder, who was breathing hard.

"Do I look alright?" Rolling Thunder cried, almost hysterically. "That freak nearly killed me!"

Simon regarded the creature in his hand, thrashing and bucking as if it had somehow caught its neck in the unyielding vice grip of a statue. He was part of that same generation of misfit monstrosities of which the Saurian was perhaps the most powerful and the best known. That sick bastard Dr. Moreau had unleashed them upon an unsuspecting world years before, and it had fallen to the heroes and first responders to track them, catch them, and put them down. Rehabilitation was not an option.

Dr. Moreau, Simon thought. H.G. Wells would have a heart attack if he knew some crazy mask took that name.

"I'll bring him to the stasis room at Echelon, in Hudson," Simon said. "Let me bring you, too. We'll get those wounds looked at."

Rolling Thunder leaned over and put his hands on his knees as he heaved and coughed. "You're going to put that thing in a cage?"

"Not exactly. We're looking for any masks and capes still around so we can find out precisely what happened," Simon said.

"Look at him," Rolling Thunder said, gesturing with one hand. "That thing doesn't think like a human. It's gone totally feral. What the hell is it supposed to tell you?"

Simon looked at Rat Bastard once again and shook him a little to get his attention. "Hey, you," Simon said. "Can you hear me? Do you know what I'm saying?"

Rat Bastard stopped struggling and relaxed. It spoke with a voice that sounded like scratching glass. "Yes."

"What are you doing here?"

"I live here."

"And what were you doing with my friend here?"

"I was searching for food, and he attacked me. Not my fault."

Simon looked at Rolling Thunder.

Rolling Thunder pointed at Rat Bastard. "He's got three murder warrants on him. I see a killer, I'm bringing him in, no matter what else is going on."

"I see," Simon said. "I'm bringing him to Echelon, to see if he can tell us anything. When we're done, he can come back here to stand trial."

"Are you serious?" Rolling Thunder said.

"Entirely," Simon said.

Rolling Thunder shrugged. "All right then."

A lightning bolt came down and lit up Rat bastard from within. His furry skin caught fire; his eyes burst as electricity erupted from them. The energy made Simon's hair stand on end, but did not hurt him. In a moment, it was over, but there was a final thunderclap echoing across the sky.

Simon smelled burning meat, and he flung Rat Bastard's smoking carcass out of his hand. Enraged, he turned to deal with Rolling Thunder, who staggered and fell over. The wounded hero turned his head to one side and vomited blood before dying. Simon scanned the body and saw a huge amount of fast-acting mutant virus all over the fallen hero. It had all come from Rat Bastard; a walking infectious wound waiting to happen. The infection was dying as fast as it was spreading, acting more like a lightning-quick poison than a true contagion. But its effects were the same as far as Rolling Thunder was concerned. It was lethal.

Jen stood next to Simon and looked upon the two bodies. "So sad," she said.

Simon flinched. Her again. "The only two people in all of Toronto, and they had to kill each other," Simon said. "I wonder if this is all we're destined for."

"Probably," Jen said with a shrug. "On a long enough timeline, the survival rate for people in our line of work is zero."

He turned to her. "That sounds like something Sigma would say."

"She did say that," Jen said. "It really had an effect on me."

"Hmph," Simon said. "I can imagine."

"There's no need to get nasty about it, Simon. You were as much a part of it as I was."

He tried to stay calm. But he so badly wanted her to be real, so he could wring her neck.

"It was your decision, Jen," Simon said. "You chose to do what you did."

"I know," Jen said sweetly. "And you chose to let it happen. Just like here. You know you could have jumped in between them rather than wait to see how the battle turned out. But you didn't."

"I didn't get here in time!"

Jen was no longer there. But her voice remained, like a whisper on the wind.

"Didn't you?"

Simon took off once more and broke the sound barrier as he left Toronto airspace. He headed south, straight for Hudson. He flew through a flock of geese while on the way up; their bodies would have exploded off him in a cloud of blood and feathers had he not rotated, pulled his arms in, and zipped between them.

Hudson closed in before him, and even though he knew he needed to go right to Echelon, he veered off course just a little bit. There was somewhere else he needed to go.

The Glenrock building still stood, unhurt by crashing airplanes, unstaggered by a structural fire on its lower floors. The terrorist scare a few years ago must have been enough to get its owners to rigorize the foundation such that it would take a small meteor to knock it over.

Simon glided to a slow and soft landing, touching down on the Glenrock building's central spire, just above its observation deck. From there, he walked up its slope, toward the four big gargoyles that extended from its corners. He went to the one where he saw Jen for the last time.

She was waiting there for him. He walked out to meet her. There was a light wind that blew her hair into a coppery halo about her face. He smiled at the sight of her. She was so beautiful. So, so beautiful.

She looked at him and the tears came easily, and he felt the world melt away in place of his memory of that day, now a whole year gone, when they were both up here after the Bayside riot had been quelled, the fires put out, and the dead put to rest.

He had been in Southeast Asia at the time doing tsunami relief when the Bayside thing went off. He'd checked in, of course, and was told that as bad as things were, there were a few hundred thousand people who needed him there right then. Besides, the rest of Echelon felt they could handle the brawl that took over the Spaghetti Bowl. They needed it, Simon thought. To know that some crises could be handled without the Praetorian's help.

It wasn't until he returned home that he really knew the full extent of how bad the Bayside riot had gotten. He had been given a briefing remotely by Ellen, of course, but it didn't become real until he arrived in Hudson and saw the bodies. Thirty-one capes. Twice that wounded. About the same for the masks. Civilian casualties, ten times the total. Three times wounded.

"It's not your fault," Simon had told Jen as she stood atop the Glenrock building. "You didn't call in the reinforcements. It just happened. Sigma has been saying it was inevitable."

"Sigma's job is to tell us what we want to hear," Jen had said through her tears. "She's the one who points us to problems we have to fix, and then explains why it's okay when we can't fix them."

She turned to face Simon, high on that skyscraper, standing out over the expanse of Hudson City, its lights forming a twinkling backdrop that outlined her.

"I saw a bus explode, Simon!" she said. "Forty kids! I saw their faces! I saw the flames!"

Simon had gone forward to hold her, but she tensed, unwilling. He went no further.

"I'm sorry I wasn't there," Simon had said.

Jen sniffed and wiped her nose with the back of her gloved hand. "You can't be everywhere," she said softly. "It's a big world, and there is only one Praetorian."

"Still," he had said, "I should have been there for you."

She shrugged. "Wouldn't have made any difference. My luck ran out. It's as simple as that."

Simon searched for the right thing to say, but all that came to his mind was that her luck couldn't run out. Luck was a purely random force with no balance or store, no will of its own and no fuel source. It was just the way the particles of the universe lined up at any given time at any given place, subject to an infinite number of variables that all had their own way of affecting each other -- except for her, the one person in the world whose personal energy field made those little variables line up in ways that her mind subconsciously knew would create an advantage for her. There was no focus to it, no need to concentrate. Fluke's luck was always on, always there, always and forever.

The bus that exploded wasn't luck. That was just something that happened, Simon had thought. It was something her luck couldn't have stopped; there was too much inevitability behind it, given how things had gone that day. Ellen could have told her that. He had tried to explain as much to her, using words he'd long since forgotten because what came after is what etched itself on his memory.

"I know it was inevitable, Simon! Don't you think I know that?" Jen was furious and distraught at the same time, and Simon kept thinking that at any moment she was going to slip off the edge. "That fight with Daisy Cutter should have lasted a few seconds! But somehow I let it go on too long. I let her call for help. I let her get out of my sight. I let all those capes and all those masks get involved, and all of the sudden, I had this bloodbath on my hands, and no way to stop it."

"Jen, you did the best you could," Simon said.

"You're right," she said. "I did do the best I could. And it wasn't enough. Because when I finally got back to Daisy Cutter and had her in a position where I could finally put her away, she took out that bus, and all those kids with it."

She lowered her head. "There's only so much we can do," she said. "Any of us. There's only so much, and there's such a big world that needs us. And there are not nearly enough of us to go around. Not with so many masks standing in our way. Not with so many people being horrible to each other. And not when we're so...so...us."

She turned around, facing the city. "We're so helpless," she said. "This whole thing we're doing is a waste of time. We're...I'm a waste of time."

Simon knew what she was building the will to do. He could have bolted out in front of her, grabbed her from the ledge, any number of things to immobilize her or stop her from doing what she intended to do, but he did none of those things. He would never have known why had she not told him.

"I know you can stop me, Simon, but you know why you won't?"

He shook his head no.

"Because even if you do, I'm going to do this. Maybe not today, and maybe not tomorrow. I'll do it on a day when you're needed in space, or when you're on the far side of the world, or when you go missing like you do for days at a time. I'll do this then, and there won't be anything you can do about it."

"Jen," he said through a tightening throat. "Don't. Please don't."

"I'm going away, Simon," she said, looking over her shoulder. "Maybe if I'm lucky, I'll see you on the street." She looked back out over the expanse of sky below her. "Or maybe not."

She fell over the edge of the precipice, her eyes closed, her hair flying behind her. Simon watched her disappear below the edge of the building, and he could not move. He could not fly, or scream, or look to see her fall. He could only stand there, frozen, petrified, empty, knowing she was awake all the way down. He wondered if she was suddenly afraid, if she instantly regretted making a choice she could not unmake. He wondered if her power would save her, if the greatest fluke of all would be the one that miraculously spared her life.

He felt his muscles obey his commands once more, and yet, it was like an invisible wall kept him from getting any closer to the side of the building where she had gone over. He slowly lifted into the sky and drifted away, across the city, going anywhere but where she had landed.

He opened his eyes, there on the building, in the present day, thinking of the time that had followed. The investigation, the media coverage, the outpouring of grief. Amid the worldwide firestorm of debate and controversy over the Bayside riot and who was really to blame for it, somehow the world found the energy to consider Fluke's death a loss greater than all of that. Simon could never quite understand it. Was it that she seemed more like one of them than any other cape in the game? Was it her good looks, her personality? That the media loved her? That she was the closest thing to a celebrity that the hero world could provide? After all, hero worship was a tricky thing, and with Fluke, the world felt as if it had finally gotten it right. And now their princess was gone.

A million other people died that day, Simon thought, the taste of acid in his mouth. And still, hers is the only death they remember.

After that, the HCPD developed leads that suggested a handful of masks might have captured Fluke and thrown her off Glenrock as revenge for the riot. Simon kept waiting for somebody to ask him about it, but everyone thought he was nowhere to be found, and so he was disqualified from any possible involvement. Somebody mentioned that it could have been suicide, and the public outrage was so great that nobody dared breathe it again, except for the most socially inept masters of conspiracy theory websites. So, finding the right mask to fit the deed was the only option left, and thus began the great shakedown. With each day that the city felt like it had gotten closer to finding Fluke's killers, the pain of the Bayside riot subsided, and the many dead and injured fell from public memory. As if it had never happened, except in the minds of those who cared to remember it. Those who felt they could not afford to forget.

They finally pinned it on three masks who were also wanted for a list of crimes too long to bother remembering. Gunsight. Ultraviolence. Howling Gail. The prosecutors put together a conspiracy based on conjecture, wishful thinking and probably more than a little fabricated evidence. The defense went through the motions of what it knew was a lost cause, and since the PD was running for higher office the next year, she wasn't about to make a last stand over three scumbags she knew should have fried for what they had already done. The public just knew these three were guilty and wanted it to be done with already.

All three were found guilty. All three sentenced to death. Simon witnessed every one as the representative of Echelon. Gunsight and Ultraviolence were ordinary enough that lethal injections worked on them. Howling Gail was put through a modified form of electrocution because she proved immune to the toxins. For each one, Praetorian looked them in the eye, and in those three terrible moments, all three of the condemned looked back at him knowing that they were innocent, that he knew the difference, and that he had said nothing about it.

He thought of them as they slowly, quietly, clinically passed out of life.

He thought of the carnage upon Bayside.

He thought of Jen on the Glenrock, and of the others over the years for whom the burden of heroism had grown so heavy they made the ultimate choice of death over life.

He looked over the vast stretches of Hudson before him, so quiet, so dark and so completely, totally empty. Devoid of people he knew in his heart were almost certain never to return. And all after some mad scientist with a little black box pushed a little red button.

He looked up into the sky, and the tears came.

I let them die, Simon thought. All of them. I let them die.

He stood where Jen had left him and looked down at the city below. He could see the ghostly form of her body lying there, looking up at him, beckoning him to follow. Come with me, Simon, and let your pain cease.

He backed from the ledge, his heart racing. "I can't," he said. "Not until I've paid for the things I've done."

11

FRIENDS CLOSE

Fifteen people stood in the courtyard of the Korovian compound, many of them looking nervously from the sky to the direction of the Echelon headquarters. They were accompanied by the entirety of Zlodic's security contingent: thirty-two clones in combat armor, each armed with four different loadouts tailored for hitting targets with different kinds of resistance.

Among the group was Harry Gleason, who still wore the outfit that had once identified him as Scrounge. Zlodic had cleaned and repaired it in the day or so since his arrival, and now that he was wearing it again, and now that he had revealed his true identity to the Regent of Korovia, Gleason somehow no longer felt like the alter ego that had defined him for so much of his life.

A man so muscular he looked like he might have some mobility problems nudged Harry roughly. "Where's he at?" the figure said with a voice at least an octave lower than the human voice box could normally produce. Gleason could practically feel the guy talking as he heard him. He knew full well who this was, and he wondered why Zlodic had brought him within the compound. The Brute was high-powered muscle for hire, an enforcer, a body man, the kind of disposable heroism masterminds so often needed when pulling one of their more elaborate plans. The Brute was the kind of guy who would pull jobs for four, maybe five years before he ended up winning a stint in lockdown for three or four times that. Exile Island was filled with people just like him, counting down their days and wondering why, if they had such special powers, they were living their lives behind bars, like any other mope who couldn't live straight.

The Brute nudged Harry again. "Hey. Wake up. Where's he at?"

Harry looked up at the Brute's head, which seemed unusually small. It probably wasn't, it was just set against so much muscle that the entire body had lost its sense of proportion. "Be cool, man," he said to the Brute. "He's coming."

"Better hurry," the Brute said. "Don't like being out in the open like this."

"That makes two of us," Harry said under his breath as he looked at the rest of the group he was in. They were all masks. Most of them he was aware of, even if he did not actually know them. The Brute fell into this category, as well as Systemic, Twin Action, Pitch Black, the Strange One and Mister Twist. Then there were a few with whom he had worked and was on good terms, like Peekaboo, Thrillseeker and the Grunger. They were all pretty similar to him: moderately powered folks just looking to live on their natural talents and stay one step ahead of the good guys. The rest were masks he didn't know, but that wasn't surprising. Since the Bayside riot, a lot of new faces and names had come into the game.

Most of them were total amateurs who didn't know their job well at all. The only thing that kept most of them on the street was that the capes had the exact same problem as they tried to refill their ranks with a legion of well-meaning rookies who were usually better at leveling a city block than they were at making a quick, clean collar without messing up the scenery.

A few of the security clones put hands to where there ears would be if they were not wearing large, high-tech helmets, then moved to take up positions looking out of the compound. Nobody else seemed to notice this but Harry, and seeing it made him nervous.

The double doors to the manor house opened, and from them walked Zlodic, wearing a battlesuit that looked like a rigid, form-fitting suit of armor that wrinkled where it should not have and stayed rigid elsewhere, though the entire thing seemed to be fashioned from a single piece of metal. This must be that Korovium I heard about, Harry thought. He estimated the suit's raw materials alone could probably float a small country for about a year.

The suit was finished with what must have been the equivalent of powder coating for a metal as finicky and resilient as Korovium. It was in the distinctive shades of green and gold and maroon that made up the Korovian flag, yet the intensity of their tones was played down, and almost seemed to disappear when viewed at an angle, when the suit's dull shine somehow blocked out all other detail.

Zlodic wore a stylized facial mask that seemed more than anything else like a slender crown linked to a framework outlining Zlodic's face. Clearly, it had been designed to look good first and to provide decent protection second.

The Regent carried no weapons, but Harry was certain he had something in store, somewhere. A guy like this doesn't suit up without a big stick to carry, he thought.

"Thank you all for gathering out here," Zlodic said. "I know the last few days have been trying ones. And I know that for some of you, your trip here has been less pleasant than you might have liked otherwise."

Harry remembered his chase into the compound. His drama had replayed itself three other times, each to the increasing annoyance of the Echelon heroes who found themselves turned away at the gate. Of them, Icarus, Section Eight and the Redeemer had been involved in two. It was only a matter of time before those guys come here whether or not they are invited, Harry felt.

The Grunger raised his hand. He looked like a homeless person, with the kind of accumulated filth and raggedy nature that only one living on the fringes of society for a long time could really build up. There was something strange about how he moved, and how the air was constantly disturbed around him, like how gasoline fumes at the pump, or like heat shimmering off of a highway. Harry wasn't quite sure of the guy's power. He just knew that it was enough to keep him on the street, and to have put four different capes in intensive care along the way. But that wasn't the most surprising thing about him.

"I think I am speaking for most, if not all, of my colleagues here when I say that I am extremely grateful for the sanctuary and hospitality you have shown us over the last thirty-six hours," the Grunger said in a perfect Eton accent. "And while you have never explained your motives, it would now appear that you require us to go into battle on your behalf. Is this, in fact, the case?" He lowered his hand and dug in his ear with a long, ragged pinky nail, pulling out a gob of wax that he sniffed at before eating.

Heads turned toward the Grunger as he spoke. A few jaws fell open. The Brute made a face of disapproval, while Zlodic raised an eyebrow and smiled. Systemic stepped forward and spoke. He was wearing what looked like an armored hazmat suit. His voice, through the mask filter, sounded vaguely robotic.

"What's the score?" Systemic said. "I mean, this is all for a bigass score, right? So let's go to work before a bunch of capes swoop down on us. I'm violating parole just being here."

The rest of the group murmured in approval. None of them were very fond of being out and exposed like this. Stories of the Echelon patrols over the last few days were more than a little hair-raising, and they all assumed that Echelon had eyes on them at this very moment.

"There is no score," Zlodic said, approaching the group so he could address them face to face. "What I have in mind is something rather different from what most of you are accustomed to."

"So...what, then?" asked Twin Action. When she spoke, her voice reverberated, as if she was saying things with two of the same voice, just a split-second apart from each other. She was providing her own harmony. Word was she could operate on two different harmonic frequencies at the same time and effectively be in two places at once. Supposedly, it was not the same kind of power as Horde, though Harry failed to see the difference.

Zlodic held his hands behind his back. "I thought we might all surrender to Echelon," he said.

The group collectively recoiled at what the Regent was suggesting. He wouldn't give the UN the time of day. Why the hell would he walk into an Echelon lockup when there was an entire city to plunder?

The Brute made a loud snorting sound and pushed some of the group aside as he muscled his way to the front. He towered over Zlodic by at least two feet.

"Can I help you?" Zlodic said, looking up.

"Who made you leader of this outfit?" the Brute said. "I mean, you don't even have any powers."

"There are those who would disagree."

"Being smart isn't a power."

"And I wondered why you called yourself the 'Brute'," Zlodic said. "By any fair measure, you are an ordinary person whose strength, endurance, and tolerance for pain far exceed that of any normal human. Wouldn't you agree?"

The Brute's oversized brows came together as he worked to follow Zlodic's line of reasoning. "Yeah."

"Try thinking of my intelligence the way you think of your strength, and you'll see why I'm..."

"This is stupid. You know what I think?" the Brute said, clenching his fists until the knuckles cracked loudly.

Zlodic kept his calm. "I can guess, but why don't you tell me?"

"I think you talk a lot, and I think people here will need a new boss once I smash you into a little sardine can. What do you think about that?"

Zlodic hit the Brute faster than anybody expected. His Korovium gauntlets buffered his hands from the impact, so the bones did not break. Yet those same gauntlets would not yield against the Brute's body, and so the punch to his sternum cracked it in half.

The Brute drew in a long, astonished gasp. He stood in place, unmoving while his eyes bugged out and fixed on Zlodic in an unbelieving stare. It was the look Zlodic fully expected, and he ignored it as he followed his first strike with a leaping kick that drove his armored toe into the Brute's temple. The Brute's skull stove in a little, visibly denting.

Zlodic spun around, following through from the kick and gracefully landing back where he started. The Brute was still standing before him, but his eyes rolled back, showing only the whites, and blood began running out of his nose. A second later, the huge body fell hard to its knees, and then pitched forward, slamming face-down.

Harry rushed to the Brute's body and put his fingers to the neck. He held them there, looking for a pulse. He looked up and shook his head no. "He's dead."

"Of course he is," Zlodic said evenly. "Had I meant to keep him alive, I would have only broken his knees."

There was the clicking of weapons as the rest of the security detail leveled their weapons at the group. Four of them grabbed the Brute's body and moved it into the gatehouse in the courtyard. All the while, Zlodic stood at ease and kept his eyes on the rest of the masks before him.

"Any other questions?" Zlodic said. "No? Then let me explain something to you all. At this moment, the world's remaining heroes are gathered in the Echelon facility across town. They have been planning to raid this compound with their total strength, and the only thing that has kept them from doing so just yet is that the Praetorian has not yet returned. When he does, you know as well as I do that there will be a small war here."

"Then bring them on!" shouted one of the unknown masks. "We can take them!" A few agreed, and the unknown, with more confidence, said again, "We can take them!"

"To what end?" Zlodic said. "For what purpose? I am certain that whatever made the rest of the human race disappear the other day, those people are not coming back."

"Ever?" said another unknown mask.

Zlodic looked right at him. "Ever."

He let the weight of that sink in for a moment.

"We are in an empty world, my friends. There are less than thirty of us left on Earth. Anybody who is left is like us. We are three days into the abyss, and what are we doing? The Echelon patrols an irrelevant city looking for criminals, and we are only too happy to oblige them by stealing and destroying whatever we please. It is pointless. Worse than that, it is mindless."

"We're not going into some cage, man," said Systemic.

"Nor am I," Zlodic said. "But I won't spend the rest of my life watching Echelon with a nervous eye. I will not allow that."

One of the guards gestured to Zlodic and made a circular motion with his left hand. Zlodic nodded in return.

"We don't have much time," he said, typing something against the back of his gauntlet, though there was no visible keyboard on it. In the distance, there was a monstrous roar. "Echelon is coming."

"Here?" said Harry. The instant he said it, he knew how stupid it sounded.

"Yes, here," Zlodic said. He was still typing something into his gauntlet. He finished, then looked up at the group. "We are villains in a world that has nothing left for us to threaten. And we are chased by heroes who have nothing left to protect. This war of ours, this endless struggle...it has to end. And it has to end now."

"Your guys don't seem to think that way," said one of the unknown masks.

"They are here to ensure that the Echelon listens to what I have to say. I am hoping they will be open to reason."

"And what if they aren't?" said Systemic.

Zlodic looked briefly at the gatehouse holding the body of the Brute. That was his answer. And they all understood.

The sound of heavy aircraft engines approached from the far side of midtown. A strange aircraft that looked like a cargo helicopter, but with stubby wings and VTOL jets, flew slowly overhead, banking as it circled. Harry looked up at it and could see the large sensor guns pointing groundward from turrets on the aircraft's chin, tail and midsection. He figured they were ultrawave guns, designed to create intense feelings of pain, or maybe alpha wave stimulators to make everybody on the ground instantly fall asleep. He had been on the receiving end of both kinds of weaponry before. He preferred the second to the first.

Zlodic looked upward as well, one hand shielding his eyes against the early daytime sunlight. He waved up at the craft with his other hand. The flyer moved back the way it had come a little, rotating in the air and lowering to the street as its landing gear extended.

The clones stepped away from the wall, obeying a silent command. Zlodic motioned with his right hand just a little, and the gates to his compound unlocked and retracted open, each of the doors collapsing into itself as it parted from the other. Within seconds, it was as if the gate was not even there. The superlifter from Echelon sat diagonally across the street, a hundred yards away. Its back clamshell doors were open, and people were filing out. Capes. At least twenty of them. Icarus, the Redeemer and Section Eight were the first on the ground. With them were Iron Will, Rushmore, the Nightingale and Sigma. The rest, Harry did not recognize. Most likely rookies. They're doing worse than we are, Harry thought.

Zlodic walked out of the compound, but he gestured to Harry to hang back.

"I would be lying if I said that I was not curious where he was going," said the Grunger. "Or what he was planning on telling all of those hero types."

"They don't look like they're in a talking mood," said Twin Action.

"No, they don't," said Systemic.

"Everybody just stay cool," Harry said. "Regent knows what he's doing."

"Regent's gonna get himself killed," said Systemic nervously. "This is gonna go Bayside. I can feel it."

"No it isn't," Harry said, annoyed. "Just shut up for a minute. Maybe you'll learn something." He turned away and looked out of the compound, to Zlodic and the group of capes. Come on, Z, he thought. Make this work.

The Saurian roared in the middle distance, and most of the capes looked in that direction and fanned out, ready for action. The Saurian was enormous now, fifteen feet tall and several tons of muscle and bone and tooth and claw. He seemed mostly humanoid, hunched over, with backwards bending legs. His head was distinctly more human than animal, however, with a line of teeth much smaller than the ones it had sported when fighting Rushmore the day before.

"YOU CALLED," the Saurian said, loudly enough to be heard in the compound. Zlodic could be seen speaking up to him, though he could not be heard. The Saurian nodded its head and said, "IF YOU SAY SO." It backed off a few long steps. The Echelon team relaxed its stance, if only a little.

Sigma and Zlodic did most of the talking in a conversation that, to Harry, seemed to last for an hour and a half. But within five minutes, their talk was over, and the Echelon crew was heading back into its aircraft. The Redeemer stood outside until the rest were inside, staring intently at the Korovian compound until Iron Will came out and put his hand on his shoulder to guide him into the craft. The Redeemer shrugged Will off with a single, violent movement and spent another few moments staring. Harry could feel his eyes burning upon him. Then, the burning ceased, and the Redeemer went into the aircraft. Its doors closed, the engines fired up, and the entire thing lifted off once more. It backed away from the Korovian facility, rotated 180 degrees, and headed back toward Echelon.

Harry watched Zlodic speak to the Saurian, who in turn looked toward Echelon and said "ARE YOU SURE." Zlodic spoke some more, and the Saurian said "YES. I

TRUST YOU." With that, the Saurian walked away, toward the southern end of midtown island; Zlodic walked back to little Korovia.

Once inside, his security clones stood down. The group of masks silently waited to hear from Zlodic.

"Well?" said Systemic. "What's the deal?"

"The deal," Zlodic said, "is that we're all going home."

"What do you mean?" asked Twin Action.

Zlodic smiled as he spoke, and tears ran from his eyes. "The war is over."

"Who won?" Harry said.

"Everybody," Zlodic said as the Echelon airlifter disappeared from view. "Everybody."

12

ENEMIES CLOSER

Over the Hudson City skyline, the airlifter hummed as it cut through the clear air. A minute later it was above Echelon Island, and slowing in for a vertical landing on the pad on top of the motor pool. After a successful touchdown, the pad itself lowered into the garage, and secondary roof tiles slid closed above it.

Once the ceiling was in place, the vehicle locked into position. It powered down and the doors opened, letting its occupants leave. The clamshell doors at the back split and flipped, and the riders stepped out in twos and threes.

The Redeemer seethed as he followed his colleagues out of the airlifter, back into the Echelon motor pool. "This is worse than stupid," he said. "This is collusion with the enemy."

Rushmore heard what he said, rotated to Teddy Roosevelt and stomped up to him. "Better stow that," he grumbled. "It's a good idea, even if came from one of them."

The Redeemer looked at Rushmore defiantly. "You think I'm afraid of you, stone man? I pity you and all those other freaks for buying into this. We're in a war that never ends unless all of them give up. That's when it ends. Not with a ceasefire. Not with some...*truce*." He said the last word like it was profanity.

"Suck it up," Rushmore said with a grin.

"We'll see what the Praetorian thinks of this when he returns," the Redeemer said, his arms crossed.

"Yeah," Rushmore said, turning his back and walking down the airlifter's clamshell doors. "We will. Now fall in."

On the flight deck of the motor pool, the airlifter's crew and passengers assembled in an informal group, all facing toward the vehicle, waiting for its pilot to address them. The cockpit hatch popped open, and Ellen climbed out. As she hit the ground, she removed the flight glasses she had been wearing, folded them and hung them inside the collar of her flightsuit.

"Everybody here heard the terms and bore witness, as we agreed," Ellen said. "Now begins the hard part."

A few of the people sighed loudly or muttered. Most of them were rookies.

"Cut the chatter, people. You all heard what the Regent suggested, so now we vote on it."

The Redeemer broke in. "We cannot vote. The Praetorian is not here."

The Nightingale leaned forward so she could turn her head and see him. "Actually, we can. He is just one vote, and we have more than enough for a quorum. This vote is both legal and binding."

"Thank you," Ellen said. The Nightingale smiled and nodded her head to her. "The truth is, we don't know where the Praetorian is. He could be back in a day, he could be back in a month. But the Regent put forth an offer we need to decide upon now, and that means we put it to a vote."

Ellen paused, scanning the group, the future unfolding before her. She could not see the way through it. It was too murky and unfixed. Anything could happen. These were the times that scared her.

"Until the effects of the Omega Event have been somehow reversed, and we are reunited with the way things were, I hereby move that we suspend the articles of the Echelon Mandate as written by the United Nations, that we waive all criminal charges, sentences and warrants in existence previous to the Omega Event, and that we make every effort to extend a hand of friendship to all other survivors, regardless of their affiliation or history."

"You mean join with the Regent's gang," the Redeemer said.

"Shut up," said Iron Will, glaring at the cowled avenger. "And don't try giving me that look of yours either. It doesn't work on me."

"That is the motion," Ellen said. "Do I have a second?"

"Second," said the Nightingale.

"Then let's vote on it," Ellen said. "All in favor of the motion, please raise your hand."

Ellen, Rushmore, the Nightingale and three of the rookies raised their hands. Iron Will saw this, and slowly raised his hand. When he did, so did Fast Forward. Vorpal, who had returned from his villain hunt shortly before being loaded into the airlifter for the flyover of the Korovian compound, seemed uncertain, and half-raised his hand until he thought better of it and let it drop.

Just then, two figures entered the motor pool; one was a young woman wearing what looked like a ballistically reinforced flightsuit and the other was an older, heavier man who looked like he could have been the uncle to anybody in the room, except Rushmore. He wore a utilitarian variant of the Echelon uniform, not entirely unlike what the Nightingale wore.

"I got your call, Sigma," said the woman as she walked briskly across the motor pool. "And I'm glad we got here in time to stop this insanity. What the hell are you thinking?"

"It's being put to a vote," Ellen said. "You care to add to it, Stratosphere?"

She looked at the raised hands and shook her head in disdain. "In favor of this? I don't think so."

"Artifex, thanks for coming," Ellen said. I trust Stratosphere told you what we're voting on?"

"I got the gist of it," said the Artifex, who removed his goggles and polished them with a pocket cloth as if they were spectacles. "We're talking about calling it quits to the whole heroes and villains thing, right? No more cops and robbers, no more chases and street fights, no more putting bad guys in lockdown, and no more us and them. Is that correct?"

Ellen nodded. "That's right."

The Artifex put his goggles back on and promptly raised his hand. "Then I'm in."

The Nightingale smiled broadly at him, while Stratosphere threw up her hands. "I should have left your fat ass back in Australia."

"When you've been in the game as long as I have, you know a good thing when you see it. And believe me, this is as good as it's ever going to get for people like us," the Artifex said.

"These people are scum!" Stratosphere shouted. "They are murderers and thieves and they are the exact opposite of everything we stand for! What kind of world will this be if there is no more right and wrong?"

"A quieter one," the Artifex said, his hand still high. "And maybe a more peaceful one, too."

"It's not my problem you got tired, old man. You should have just retired and left the real work to those of us who still have the strength for it," Stratosphere said. The Redeemer nodded in approval, as did a few rookies.

"I think you've made your point," Ellen said to Stratosphere. She looked around the group and counted their votes. There were eight. "All right, everyone. Drop your hands. All opposed?"

Stratosphere, the Redeemer, Icarus and Section Eight all raised their hands without hesitation, as did two of the Echelon rookies. Three more rookies voted against, but each more unsure of his or her vote than the last.

"Vorpal, you voting with us?" said Stratosphere expectantly. She sounded more than a little annoyed that he had come so close to voting in favor of Sigma's proposition.

Vorpal shook his head no. "I can't. Sorry, Stratosphere...I just can't. I have to abstain on this one."

Two of the rookies who voted against looked at Vorpal, then at each other, and slowly lowered their hands. The vote against went from ten to eight.

"Are you three sure?" Ellen asked. "None of you wish to vote against?"

Vorpal shook his head no. So did the two rookies.

"Very well," Ellen said. "The vote is ten to eight. The motion passes."

"What?" said the Redeemer. "They cannot abstain! There is no voting on an issue such as this!"

"Their vote was not to vote," Iron Will said. "I don't like it any more than you do. But that's the way it is. Sigma, you want to put the word out to Regent and his crew?"

Ellen nodded. "I'll let them know."

Stratosphere stepped between Ellen and Will. She was almost nose to nose with Ellen. "I don't know what kind of stunt you think you're getting away with, but the Praetorian will never let this stand."

"I think you underestimate him," Ellen said. "Plus, I can see things you cannot. I know he will allow this."

Stratosphere looked skeptical. "Keep telling yourself that, Sigma. In the meantime, those masks are not coming here. I don't care if we're all friends now or not, not a single one of those people is setting foot in my home. I have lost too many friends to them and their kind to live alongside them now."

"It's a big world that's suddenly gotten a whole lot bigger," Ellen said. "I'm sure we can all find ways to not get in each other's way. Excuse me." She angled past her and walked out of the motor pool. Stratosphere half-turned to watch her leave, and as she did, she was joined by the Redeemer, Section Eight and Icarus.

"The Regent got to her," Icarus said.

"And they say I'm the crazy one," Section Eight said.

"None of this matters," the Redeemer said. "The war isn't over. It's just going underground. Who is with me?" He put out his fist.

Stratosphere put her hand on top of it. So did Section Eight and Icarus.

"Then it's settled," the Redeemer said. "Our first target is the Regent. We take him out, he loses his grip on Sigma. With one collar, the masks lose their leader and so do the collaborators."

They parted their hands. "I need a drink," said Stratosphere. "The wet bar in the rec lounge better still be stocked or I'm going to break some heads."

Elsewhere in the headquarters, Ellen entered the watchroom, where she did all of her precognitive monitoring, and sat in her chair, suddenly feeling exhausted. She closed her eyes and exhaled slowly, letting her tension escape. She ran her fingers against her bald head, massaging her temples. God, that was close, she thought. If Vorpal hadn't abstained...and why did he do that, anyway? That's not like him. He's always been the loose cannon, the guy we had to hold back so he wouldn't kill some mask too slow to get out of the way. He even cut off Threshold's hands thinking it would rob him of his powers. Maybe he's had a bellyful of killing and sees a chance to live the quiet life for once.

The quiet life, Ellen thought. Not the sort of thing any of us ever saw for ourselves. It's not perfect, and it isn't glorious. But it'll work.

"You have some explaining to do," said a voice, deep and strong and angry.

Ellen's eyes snapped open. The Praetorian was standing in front of her in the monitoring room. He suddenly seemed ten feel tall, and his thick arms were crossed. Ellen noticed that his eyes were red. She had once seen a mercenary fire a .45 pistol right into his eye, and he didn't even blink. He's been crying, she thought. Only explanation. But over what? Surely not this.

"Where have you been?" Ellen said, rising from her chair.

"Around," Simon said. "I had a few more places to check before I came back. I didn't think I was needed. I see that I was wrong."

"I take it that you've spoken to Stratosphere and the Redeemer."

"No, I spoke with Iron Will and Rushmore. Rushmore seemed pretty satisfied with this little coup you think you have pulled off. Iron Will, not as much." Simon shook his head in disbelief. "Ellen, I'm stunned. You of all people...collaborating with him? With the Regent?"

"Look, Simon, you don't know all of the details. Zlodic..."

"Don't use his name in my presence," Simon said. "Not like that. He doesn't get that right. Not after all he has done."

"None of that matters anymore, Simon. That's the whole point. Everyone is gone. There is only us. And we can either choose to battle until we're all dead, or we can take this opportunity to start over for ourselves."

"Start over?" Simon said. "And do what? The war is all we have ever known. It is all I am. You too, for that matter. And what of Zl--the Regent? Are we to assume that he will suddenly no longer wish to conquer the world? Or put humanity on a path to extinction?"

"Yes," Ellen said. "We are to assume precisely that. The world he wanted to conquer no longer exists. The humanity he wanted to destroy has gone missing. The things that made him dangerous no longer do. Just like how the things that made people like Vorpal a necessary evil no longer exist."

"And so heroes become villains and villains become heroes. Is that it?"

"Only if we can't figure out how to live outside of our capes and masks, Simon. Look me in the eyes and tell me you haven't dreamed of a day when you could just be, and not have to worry about trying to save an entire world bent on tearing itself apart."

"I will not be part of this delusion," Simon said. "And I will not let it go on any longer. There are six billion people who are lost out there somewhere, and who need us to bring them home."

"Simon," Ellen said, "Did it ever occur to you that maybe we're the ones who are lost?"

He said nothing.

"I understand how you feel," she said to him, softly. "I do. But you have to understand that we voted on this. We decided as a group, and as a group, we gave Zlodic and every other survivor a chance to start things over again. Clean slate. No more good guys, no more bad guys. Just a bunch of people who have been fighting a war for so long that they forgot what it was really about."

"And what's that?"

She rubbed the back of her head. "I don't know. But how about we find out?"

Simon tensed his jaw. "I have to go," he said.

"You know where to find us," Ellen said. "And you know you are always welcome here."

Simon left the monitoring room and walked slowly through the halls of Echelon, trying to grasp the magnitude of what had just happened. He thought of the Regent's cunning and how, of all his many plots, this one was easily the most insidious, the most damaging. For when the people come back, Simon thought, we capes will still know that there was a time when we decided to leave our posts and join with the enemy. There will be no going back to the war after this, Simon thought. Regardless of what happens, some of our best and brightest have been compromised. One day, we will have to square with that.

"I think you were a little hard on Ellen, don't you?" said Jen, next to him.

Simon instantly looked to his side. Jen was walking with him, still dressed as Fluke. She looked happy, how he preferred to remember her.

"No," he said as he moved through Echelon's winding hallways, back to street level and the campus outside. "What she did was totally out of line. And she would never have thought of it had the Regent not put the idea in her head."

"I think you're just upset because he came up with it first," Jen said. "To be honest, it sounds pretty good to me."

"Of course it does. You're a figment of my imagination."

"Well, you don't have to be rude about it," she said, pouting a little. "Would it really be so bad if everybody just gave up the great game and tried to live with each other for once?"

"No, but that's assuming Zlodic and his followers are genuine. Can you imagine them all hanging up their masks and farming or painting pictures for the rest of their lives? I can't. It's ludicrous."

"Everything is different now, Simon," Jen said. She stopped and he felt her fingers on his face, gently turning him toward her. "Look at me. Everything is different. In your heart, you know it. Let it go, Simon."

She looked at him with moist eyes. "Let it go."

"I can't," he said. "It's all I have."

"Then you're as lost as I was," she said as she turned to walk down a different path than he. "But it's not too late to find a way out. You just have to look for it."

Simon stood by himself in the hallway, looking off into space as her words hung in his ears. He could still feel the lightness of her fingertips against his impenetrable skin. When he snapped out of it, he noticed that she was gone.

He continued upwards, to the surface, and once there, he noticed that nobody was around. He sensed they had all headed into midtown, where he could hear the earth rumbling, concrete fracturing, steel rending and glass breaking.

"I knew it," he said, bolting into the sky, ready to visit furious havoc on the masks, who couldn't wait even an hour before abusing the privilege of the idiotic truce Ellen had struck with the Regent.

Once in the park, however, he noticed that it was no mask that was creating all of the noise and disruption. Rather, it was the Artifex, standing on a tall stone column of his own making, his hands out and moving, like one conducting an orchestra. Before him, the land of the Midtown Park was obeying his every command; huge rock upthrusts were slowly coming to the surface, thousands of tons of soil churning and flowing like water, pieces of skyscrapers tearing away from themselves and floating over to the park to stand in line like workers awaiting orders.

Simon watched in fascination as the Artifex did his work. Usually, he had been called upon to conduct emergency repairs somewhere; he was the reason why Hudson did not look like a smoldering post-war ruin on any given day. No matter how bad a throwdown got nor how much collateral damage was caused, the Artifex could make things right, simply by remembering how they had been before. In those rare instances where he could not remember, his sense of architectural design and innovation always left the new building looking far better than it had previously. At least, Simon recalled, there had never been any lawsuits over it, and in this day and age, that was saying something.

Over the course of an hour, the Artifex's work took shape, and what had once been a large stretch of forested wilderness in the heart of the world's greatest city now was a village of inviting stone cottages arranged in a circular pattern, with streets like spokes running between them, and the areas in between filled with green lawns and gardens, and lines of trees shading every lane. In the heart of it all was a large covered plaza, an old-style meeting hall with concentric rows of seats, looking like some cross between a Roman amphitheater and a public meeting house from colonial New England. Simon liked it.

Somehow, the Artifex moved and shifted the remains of the surrounding park into such a pattern that they never betrayed that they had ever been disturbed. Roads led from the village to the rest of the city, curving and winding through the forest in ways that left a direct enough path to those willing to take it, but leaving no direct line of sight connecting the village to the rest of the city.

Standing around the base of the Artifex's column were the members of Echelon, much as Simon had expected. Keeping a respectful distance on the far side of what was becoming the Village, Simon could see the Regent, in his suit of armor, flanked by his motley crew of marauders, psychotics and assassins. The Saurian was there, huge as always, but looking more human than ever before. Now he was merely an oversized man with scaly green skin and clawed fingernails.

Simon had half a mind to fly into them at full speed and tear as many apart as he could before whatever secret weapon the Regent had in mind went off, incapacitating him. Another time, he told himself. There will have to be another time.

The finishing touch was the city's skyline, which still stood over the Village and imposed the atmosphere of Hudson upon it. The Artifex put his hands out to the sides and moved them in slow, circular patterns that led to the entire Village descending into the earth, and the edges of the park rising up. Where there had been only wooded flatland, now there were forested ridges that stood between the park and its city, and where the Village had once occupied a meadow, now it was in the center of a new valley, hidden from view from the great city beyond, which was itself hidden from view from those within the Village.

Finally, the Artifex finished, and he let his arms hang at his sides. The members of Echelon gave up a cheer and applause for their exhausted builder, who let Rushmore lift him off the column and carry him on his shoulder. Simon watched as Ellen led the members of Echelon down the path through the park that led into the Village. As she went, Zlodic did the same, and his contingent followed him into the Village. Both groups met in the center, and Simon had no choice but to fly closer to listen, to observe, and to wait to see what would happen next.

If I am there, it will go differently, he thought. I need only be close enough to act if I am needed, nothing more.

"I see you are as good as your word," Simon heard Zlodic say to Ellen.

"I am," Ellen said. "And you as good as yours?"

Zlodic nodded, and he hit a clasp on the side of his suit that let his armor detach and fall away in large segments. He stepped out of it, and held his hands to the sides, and turned around. See? his motions said. Nothing on me. Nothing to hide.

Simon scanned the air for signs of the tailored nanoweapons Zlodic was so fond of, but the air was clean. So was Zlodic himself. Nothing on him that suggested he was amped up or rigged to detonate something. It had seemed possible that he might try some kind of doomsday move to kill everybody on the planet but himself.

"Welcome to the Village," Ellen said and extended her hand.

"Thank you," Zlodic said. "My friends and I are glad to be here." He turned and looked knowingly in Simon's direction. "You have known me as the Regent, but from this day forth, that name will mean nothing to me. You will know me as Zlodic Viriskoya, scion of Korovia and fourth son of the House of Vladistadt.

"Ellen," she said with enthusiasm. "Ellen Dubinovich."

There was a long, awkward silence as both sides looked at each other, sizing up the other half. Finally, Rushmore stepped forward. Everybody tensed.

"They call me Rushmore. It's the only name I've got," he said, his head rotating to George Washington. "And that's no lie."

Somebody on Zlodic's side laughed out loud, and the effect was contagious. Soon everybody was cracking up over the jibe, and lines broke on both sides as people stepped forth to remove their masks and their cowls and their hoods and their helmets. One by one, they introduced themselves by their real names to people they might have fought for years, but never gotten to actually know. Melinda. Garvin. Katsui. Phil. Barbara. Mike. Dan. Gwendolyn. Luz. Maria. Twende. Stefan. Khalid. Ruth.

There were those who hung back, of course. The Redeemer and Stratosphere were especially slow to join the gathering, and even slower to reveal their true names. But the groups had come together, and as much as Simon wanted to believe that what he was seeing wasn't really happening, he knew that it was. Ellen was right. Zlodic was on the level. And now, even more than the days before, everything was different.

He sat down on the hilly rise overlooking the Village and watched the mass greeting unfold with mixed feelings of awe and disappointment. After so much hardship, after so much loss, it was finally over, this war that had defined them all. And all with something as simple as a handshake. Who knew it could be so damned easy?

He felt Jen sitting beside him, and she rested her head on his shoulder. "Isn't that great?" she said, pointing to the Village. "I love happy endings."

"This is no ending," Simon said.

"Then what is it?" Jenny asked.

"A mistake," Simon said. "And I won't be a part of it."

He stood and closed his eyes, letting his power build around him before he launched from the earth, exploding upward into the sky. He flew straight up, moving so fast that contrails followed him as he went. Finally, he broke the sound barrier, leaving a distant boom of thunder high above the Village and everyone within it.

For a moment, they all looked skyward to the noise, some shading their eyes against the sun, looking for the one who left them. He was gone.

TO BE
CONTINUED

CPSIA information can be obtained
at www.ICGtesting.com
Printed in the USA
FSOW03n1609140416
19201FS

9 781936 519248